MIDNIGHT CLEAR

ANGEL'S LEGACY
BY CARMEN GREEN

HOME FOR THE HOLIDAYS
BY LESLIE ESDAILE

Genesis Press, Inc.

Indigo Love Stories

An imprint of Genesis Press, Inc.
Publishing Company

Genesis Press, Inc.
P.O. Box 101
Columbus, MS 39703

ISBN-13: 978-1-58571-357-8
ISBN-10: 1-58571-357-0
Manufactured in the United States of America

First Edition 2000
Second Edition 2009

Visit us at www.genesis-press.com or call at 1-888-Indigo-1

MIDNIGHT CLEAR

Angel's Legacy   *1*
  by Carmen Green

Home for the Holidays   125
  by Leslie Esdaile

ANGEL'S LEGACY

BY CARMEN GREEN

Most folks never heard of Mystic Ridge, and if truth be told we like it just like that. You can't find it on the map and if you drive too fast you'll likely go right by it. But if you make that turn, the one down by the lake, between the thicket of bushes and trees, you'll ease right on into Mystic.

Legend has it that Mystic Ridge has been around since the beginning of time, that our ancient ancestors walked across these lands, swam in these waters, setting our course, defining our destiny. More than four hundred years ago, slaves found the route to Mystic and settled here, bringing their sorrows, joys, traditions, and hope. Some say the ancestors still live in the mountains, sit by the rivers and walk along the paths, watching over all who come here, casting their spells and making mischief. I believe it's true. There's something real special about this place. Real special. Some believe the stories, some don't. But I been 'round long enough to know they be true. Yessir. I'll never forget the winter that it snowed. First time in nearly five years. Yessir, all kinds of havoc unfolded in Mystic. Knew it was coming, too. If you want to set a spell, I'll tell you all about it.

You see, it all started with a big rumbling up in the sky, like it was going to open up. Oh, yeah, I remember that year...

ANGEL'S LEGACY

Queen Nefertiti glanced over at her esteemed queenly counterparts, Sheba and Dahia, and waited for them to join her.

"Queens," Nefertiti said, "Come. Time is of the essence. We must make a decision as to whom we will bestow the legacy of leadership, spirit and wisdom."

Dahia, who fought her last battle in 702 A.D., stalked toward Nefertiti, agile as the fiercest lion of her day.

How different we all are, Nefertiti thought. While she was tall, slightly sun-kissed and preferred silk to lamb's wool, Dahia's color resembled the deepest shade of earth. And Dahia preferred her metal breast-plate above any fine fabric.

Sheba, on the other hand, was a natural woman. Adorned with rings on her ears, neck, and arms, she possessed the stride of a goddess with her beauty further enhanced by the pride she took in being a woman.

Quite an odd group, Nefertiti thought, as the metal of Dahia's breastplate caught on a ray of heaven's light.

Sheba reached Nefertiti's side and adopted her at-ease stance.

"We must succeed this time," Dahia commanded. "Our future depends on it. Sheba! Have you narrowed down the selections?"

Makeda, the Queen of Sheba, considered Dahia with an arched brow and a gentle but firm tone. "Calm yourself, sister. You are no longer on the battlefields of Aures issuing orders to your men. Yes, I have done my job. Sit. I am ready."

Queen Nefertiti, known for her beauty and intelligence, waited for the queens to gather around before grasping their hands.

The resistance was real as Dahia, who had slain men with those hands in her effort to save Africa from Arab invasion, struggled with the notion that her hands were needed for another type of battle.

Sheba, as exquisite as her name, struggled less, but Nefertiti could see the wariness in her eyes.

"Give us her name," Nefertiti said to Sheba.

"Our chosen one is Angelina Snowden."

Dahia tugged to get free but was unsuccessful. She stopped for a moment. "Did we not try with her mother, Ruth Snowden?"

"Correct." Sheba's self-assurance was unconvincing to the warrior priestess.

"Then why try again with the descendant of a failure?"

"Have we not all failed at one time or another? I fell from my husband's grace before his death. You,

Dahia, were slain on the battlefields of your beloved country, and Sheba bore David by a King she did not marry."

Sheba drew herself up. "That is a regret I care not to discuss." Nefertiti didn't intend to engage that discussion either. Sheba could go on and on about Solomon.

"We are here to instill the legacy," Nefertiti said. They each turned to view moments of Angel's life. But it wasn't birthday parties they watched. They studied her fights, tests of her character, moments of failures.

"She's the one." Sheba saw Angel's future sons and smiled. "So like my David. Strong. Men of God."

Dahia saw her strength. "She will fight for her land and her family."

Nefertiti saw her wisdom. "Although beautiful, she will not rely on looks to enhance her success. She is smart. She has spirit. She is the chosen one. This legacy belongs to Angel."

Images flashed of a young Angel's numerous spankings for displays of stubbornness. A tear streaked her cocoa brown face as her father whipped her.

"Look at her," Dahia said in a hushed tone. "She is a warrior. He cannot break her spirit."

Nefertiti applied gentle pressure to Dahia's hand. "She survived. Look at her. She is love." They watched as the young Angel grew into womanhood and experienced her first love. They watched her fall in love and viewed her making love.

Sheba cocked her head. "They still do that? Solomon and I invented that move."

The queens smiled, indulging Sheba's fantasy. They each had invented moves of their own. Sheba continued. "She has traveled the world and has seen the atrocities perpetuated against our people and experienced the breakdown of our own self love. Yet, she is not bitter. Angel is the chosen one. Nefertiti?"

"Yes, dear one?"

"What say you?"

Nefertiti regarded her counterparts. "We have chosen in the past and failed. The legacy must be instilled before the turn of the millennium. The woman chosen will be responsible for restoring wisdom, leadership and spirit to the people of African descent. If the legacy is not instilled, our race will never know true unity. Angelina Snowden is our last chance. The Kings have chosen another male who will mate and marry Angelina. But they must mate and marry while in love, queens, or we have lost our opportunity. If we are of one accord, then let us link fingers, palm to palm where the lifelines meet and cast down the legacy."

Nefertiti held up her left hand and linked with Dahia's right. Sheba's right linked with Dahia's left and Sheba's left linked with Nefertiti's right. The circle was complete. The whispered prayers in the native language of each rose into a swell of adulation, hope and praise.

Power emanated from the trio, and from the soles of their feet to the tips of their hair, each shook with the pride of their African heritage. Nefertiti moved first, bringing her and Dahia's hands into the center of the group. They clasped together in a show of solidarity and spoke in unison.

"Father, you ordained us queens, but it is you we give the honor and praise. We are one in the spirit, one in you and we pass on our ordination to another of your children. Angel," they said in unison, "is the chosen one. We give her what you gave to us."

"Spirit," said Dahia.

"Wisdom," said Nefertiti.

"Leadership," said Sheba.

"Love," they said in unison. "We pass it on."

Tingles passed among the three and each opened her eyes to view Angel traveling in her car on a long dark stretch of road.

Her car jolted suddenly and came to an abrupt stop. Each held her breath. Then the car started to move again. And they breathed a collective sigh of relief.

Dahia and Sheba rose from their kneeleing position and watched Angel as she drove into her hometown of Mystic Ridge, Maryland.

"She's got it," Sheba said.

Dahia harrumphed. "Let's see what she will do with it."

"Angel will succeed," Nefertiti predicted, still on her knees, her hands clasped. She whispered a fervent prayer and joined the other two as the waiting began.

CHAPTER ONE

The long, dark desolate road snaked ahead of Angelina Snowden, winding her closer to her hometown of Mystic Ridge, Maryland.

She pushed back strands of her spiral-curled hair and guided her brand new candy-apple red BMW convertible through the clear night, keeping one eye on the road and the other on the hand held CD player remote.

The car had been an unmitigated indulgence when, she, as the first black executive for the Crown Company, had won the Dyer account, and it served as a reminder as to why she'd driven nearly two thousand miles from Los Angeles to Mystic Ridge.

Convincing the powers that be of the four hundred-year-old town that change is good would take some doing, but who better than she to do it? The Dyer Corporation was known for reviving the economy of small towns and according to her mother and other locals, Mystic Ridge was ripe for change.

Tall smoky columns of fog appeared suddenly and stretched toward the dark sky. The long white swirling pillars surrounded the car and it rocked as she drove deeper into the smoke screen.

Easing off the accelerator, Angel let her imagination run away for a moment and gave in to the first question that entered her mind: What lay behind this great white gateway?

Nothing in her life had ever been so...mystical before.

She chuckled at the irony but caught her breath as her body started to tingle, going hot and cold in a full body flush.

Suddenly the car shook violently, casting her sideways.

In an act driven by instinct, she grabbed the steering wheel, planted both feet on the brakes and brought the vehicle to a screeching halt. Angel's heart raced, her palms sweat and her body shivered as her breath came in drawn-out gasps.

She opened her eyes to see a navy blue sky, dotted with glistening stars and a luminescent crescent moon.

The clouds were gone, the pillars of fog nonexistent. The flush that had flooded her body with sensation had been replaced by a warm sunk-in-the-tub feeling.

What had just happened?

Angel looked at herself in the rearview mirror.

Nothing was different. She didn't have any strange markings to indicate she was a case for the "X-Files", nor had she entered a new "Stargate" dimension.

She was on the highway, twenty-five miles from her mother and step-father's house—at a complete standstill.

White headlights on the other side of the tree-lined barrier continued to flow, but no car had come near her in the past half-hour. Angel decided not to chance fate or her safety and got underway.

After a few miles of riding in tense silence, she decided the car had malfunctioned and needed to be reprogrammed. The dealer would fix it when she got back to L.A.

Reassured, she pressed the gas pedal.

An ethereal voice, strong and distinct filled the car. "You are the chosen one."

Stomping on the brakes, Angel jumped from the vehicle, her mouth open in a frightened scream.

Who was speaking?

She grabbed her face, looking around for rescue, or any living soul to verify what she'd just experienced.

No one came. Minutes passed as she fought to regain control of herself. In the night air, her breath puffed a small cloud and her ringlet curls flapped into her eyes.

Angel stared at her car.

The driver side door gaped open and the bell dinged intermittent warnings. This is insane, she told herself repeatedly. I'm in the middle of the road, scared because my car talked.

Who'd believe me?

Suddenly the weight of all that had happened rushed over her and she promised herself to never repeat this incident to another living soul. Not even her mother who used to tell the most bizarre stories about…Angel swallowed. Being chosen.

People in Mystic Ridge chalked up her mother's tales to a 'rough time' when her first husband was killed in Viet Nam, but Angel sensed what they said behind closed doors before she'd married Luther.

Angel knew if she told anyone what had happened, her credibility would be shot and she'd never convince the town folk to allow Dyer to build a large variety store in Mystic Ridge.

Gathering her courage, she took tentative steps past the rear bumper and finally slid her foot, then the rest of her body into the car.

Familiar music from Yolanda Adams's CD began to play and Angel tried to swallow in her dry throat. I knew I should have flown. Twenty-four hours on the road would make anybody hallucinate.

A feeling of calm stole over her, washing away her fear.

Angel put the pedal to the floor and sped the last twenty miles to her mother's house.

~

"Why did you do that?" Sheba demanded of Dahia. "You intentionally tried to scare her."

Dahia looked unconcerned as she put her fists on her hips and planted her feet in a wide stance. "A warrior priestess should be challenged."

"This is the year 2000. She is not a warrior priestess. She is a modern woman challenged with saving a race. Do not spook her again."

Dahia advanced, her expression provoking. "And what will you do if I do?"

Sheba tilted her head to the side, her gaze no less challenging. "I will command the locust to invade your chambers and eat your eyes out while you sleep. Once they gain entry, they will suck on your capillaries, and eventually chew out your heart. When God sees you again, you will be an eyeless, heartless old woman who—" Sheba stared at her counterpart, "has rust on her breastplate."

Dahia grabbed the metal at her chest and staggered back.

Smug, Sheba walked away.

"Are you two finished?" Nefertiti asked, biting back a laugh at Dahia's drained expression.

"I am done," Sheba said confidently.

"You are insane. That is what you are." Dahia joined the ladies as they watched the reunion of Angel and her family.

"Behave, queens," Nefertiti said. "Our purpose is higher than tests." She gave Dahia a stern look, then shifted her gaze to Sheba. "And control. Peter and Angel will meet soon. The real work has yet to begin. We must remain of one accord. Agreed?"

Dahia's chin lifted and Sheba slanted a compromising gaze at her rival. "Agreed. But she must control herself."

"I am the queen of ten thousand men!"

"Dahia!" Nefertiti could feel her patience wearing thin. "Fine," Dahia finally conceded. "I am bored."

All three focused their attention on Angel and finally caught a glimpse of Peter.

"He's handsome," Sheba said with the heat of a woman who still desired after one hundred thousand years.

Dahia cast a knowing look at her. "He is quite a man. The kings have chosen well. Shall we begin our counsel?"

All three reclined on lounging clouds and awaited the reunion of Peter and Angel.

CHAPTER TWO

Peter Richland strolled along Main Street's planked walkway, absorbing bits of life in the town that had been his home since his birth.

The weather was sunny and warm for the early November morning, and his shadow rolled across the weathered wooden sidewalk as he passed the Apothecary, Meadows Hardware store, Franklin's Antique Shop and Bunny's Beauty Salon.

Peter cast his gaze skyward when a flock of ducks flew overhead in a perfect V formation. From the park, children's voices floated toward him on a breeze, and based on the excitement level, he knew the elders had their hands full.

He took a moment and closed his eyes against the sunshine.

Wheat, yeast, butter, and spices scented the fall air and made his mouth water, while catapulting him on a dipping wave of nostalgia.

The pace and smell and feel—this was Mystic Ridge. Quiet, fragrant and unchanged by time, yet modern enough to stay afloat in the techno-crazy world.

Crossing the street, he headed toward the fourth generation owned Clay general store and slowed as Miss Lula Mae Clay stepped from the archway with her straw broom. When he was a child, he used to be scared out of his wits because Miss Lula Mae could make a pit bull cower. She still possessed that ability, but Peter was grown now, and they'd developed a mutual respect. Her daughter Maureen and her husband Will ran the store now, but Miss Lula Mae still came to work every day.

"Mornin', Miss Lula Mae. Beautiful day, isn't it?"

She arched her ninety-year-old eyes up to the sky and squinted. "The sun ain't been this bright since 1933. Course with it being the Great Depression and all, nobody but us po' folk noticed the sun at all. Just a regular day to us."

He chuckled, but didn't doubt her word.

She swatted at the dirt. "Heard a bit o' news, Petey."

Peter leaned against an old Ford truck parked diagonally in front of the store, and settled in for a spell.

"Care to share?" He expected to hear about her great-granddaughter Linda's latest pregnancy but the news had already spread. Darlene at the Apothecary had shared that little nugget of information about fifteen minutes ago. Still, he waited with polite interest. As the town council president, he was expected to listen and know the happenings in each of their lives.

Lula Mae swept vigorously for a moment then stopped just as abruptly. "Angelina Snowden done hit home. Arrived in the middle of the night. Her mama was up early buying some shrimp and fifty pounds of crabs."

Peter's heart hammered against his ribs and he wiped his mouth. "Shrimp, huh," he managed to say, his mind reeling.

Ruth's gumbo was renowned in these parts but when her daughter, Angelina, left fifteen years ago, so had Ruth's desire to cook.

A greater question pressed in on him and he let it flourish. What was Angelina doing home, and why hadn't he heard about it until after she'd arrived?

"Course Ruth and Luther are planning a welcome home party at their farm tonight."

"What time?" he said blandly, not knowing why he asked such an inane question.

"Same time as always, son. Dusk. Weren't you two thinking of jumping the broom at one time?"

Peter inhaled and let it out slowly. So this is what having Angelina home would do. Dredge up the painful past. "We were young and foolish."

Lula Mae giggled like a schoolgirl. "Those were the best of times." Her voice softened. "You need to go and show her what she missed out on. Young, strapping buck such as yourself. It's her loss, Petey."

The vote bolstered his confidence and confirmed his good sense. He and Angelina were old history. She'd left town a lifetime ago and had never looked back. But memories of her lingered like the sweet taste of cranberry tea. "I expect they can have a party without me, Miss Lula Mae. I have lots of town business to attend to."

Peter didn't ever compare himself to others, but he imagined the type of man Angelina would now be attracted to.

Probably some Ivy League, loafer-wearing brotha who wouldn't know a wheelbarrow from a tractor.

She was a corporate professional who undoubtedly earned good money and had a lot to show for her hard work. She probably made as much as ten of the citizens of Mystic Ridge put together. He was no closer to corporate America than he was to becoming the Mayor of Saturn. Sure he ran Mystic Ridge, but his suit of armor was dusty jeans, not hundred dollar suits. "I won't have time to stop by."

Lula Mae swatted him with the broom. "You know what they say about he that protests too much. The day you ain't got time to visit old friends and see what brought them home, is the day this town begins to die. If you don't go, how will I know what went on, Petey? I can't get around like I used to and if I do go, they sho' don't want me to show my knees and start dancing. Naw, they don't."

The image made him chuckle. Pulled by an unknown lure, he felt himself changing his mind. Peter grappled with his indecision. This was a first. He always made decisions and stuck with them, but even as he wanted to resist, he heard himself say, "All right. I'll go. Just for you."

Miss Lula Mae hugged his frame, although he towered a half dozen inches over the woman who used to stand a statuesque five foot ten. How could he deny this sweet old lady? Miss Lula Mae represented the essence of Mystic Ridge and he couldn't let her down. Could he? "I'll have a full report on Monday."

"You do that. And pass along my respects. I got to get back inside and take my nap. The chil'ren will be home from school in a few hours. I got to have my wits about me to deal with that lot."

"Have a good one."

Lula Mae passed Maureen, who stopped shelving bottles of syrup bearing Mystic Ridge's name, to wave at him.

Peter continued on his daily stroll and heard the news again and again. Angelina Snowden was back.

Back in his office, his first cousin and secretary, Brenda, stuck her head in his doorway. Brenda was one of those relatives people used one word to describe. Different. Her most recent thing was to shave her head completely bald. She had slightly bugged eyes, which were further enhanced by the roundness of her head.

Peter just looked at her and prepared to be swept away by her fast-talking mouth.

"Did you hear? Angelina Snowden is back. I wonder why she's here? Been so long since I last saw her." She tugged the tire around her waist. "I hope she got fat like the rest of us. Do you suppose something is wrong with Ruth? Maybe Angelina is the one sick."

Peter massaged his sun-bronzed forehead. "Don't you have anything else to do besides mind Ruth's business?"

Brenda eyed him strangely. "When aren't you up for town gossip? Honey, for your information, I have plenty to do. Ruth is having a party for Angelina and I'm going. Can I leave? Nobody is coming to see you."

"What's that supposed to mean?" Affronted, he lined up his Bic pens then straightened his Post-it note pads. In truth, today was slow, but there was always something to do. He pulled out a stack of invoices. These had to be approved, signed and mailed.

"Peter, quit fooling yourself. This ain't Alexandria or Wilmington. The only people that called today were Charlotte and Rudy from the edge of town and they wanted to complain about the stop sign you told Oscar to put up near their road. They said nobody comes out that way so why have a sign." She twirled her finger in the air. "Whoop-dee do."

Peter rubbed his cap from his head. "Did you say you were leaving?"

"I sure did. You coming to Ruth's?" Brenda talked while she packed her satchel with her lunch containers. "Let the past go and come see Angelina. It's been a long time. Do you think one of them is sick?"

Ruth wasn't sick. He'd just seen her about a week ago at Clay's. "No, I think she's just home to visit her mother."

"Well, my second cousin Bertha on my father's side thinks you're cute."

Bertha was six feet four and wore more hair on her face than he. "How fast are you leaving?"

Brenda grabbed her bag and gave her head a resigned shake. "You're alone because you've got a dry personality, Peter." With affection in her voice she said, "See you tomorrow."

Brenda's car rumbled to a start and faded in the distance.

Thankful for the silence, Peter gave her words serious consideration.

Did he indeed have a dry personality? Is that why he and Angelina never hooked up? Is that why he at thirty-three wasn't married when all his brothers and male cousins were in meaningful relationships? Had his supposed personality flaw kept him from experiencing the joy of having a family of his own?

Peter tried to laugh at the insecure notions. His voice cracked and he injected some bass until the laughter bloomed full and rich. Much better. I'm not married because I'm not ready to be married.

He finished the invoices and dragged out some zoning requests and didn't resurface until after the sun had set. The party was in full swing by now.

He tried not to think about what Angelina would look like, but he couldn't help it.

She had been gorgeous as a young woman; she could only be extraordinary now. His body stirred at the memories of him and Angelina together. They'd managed to balance wit with intelligence and pleasure with control. They'd often refrained from fulfilling the desires of their flesh, but...

Sometimes, Angelina just made him so hot, his craving for her had to be sated. He wondered if they would still generate such heat.

Peter looked down at the zoning requests and shoved them back in the drawer. There was only one way to find out.

CHAPTER THREE

Angel quietly closed the front door of her mother's plantation style home, headed around the wraparound porch and toward the back swing. In search of solitude, she ducked past an open window where her step-father Luther and aunt Dolly sat talking and eating.

The reunion had been a nice idea, but even as her mother had paraded endless relatives past her, *and* she'd become reacquainted with friends she hadn't seen in years, Angel found herself looking for the one person who hadn't come.

Settling on the swing, she shoved into a gentle wind, leaned back and let the cool breeze nip at her disappointment.

Since arriving home, life as she'd known it had ceased to exist. Almost immediately, she found herself letting go of the intense California pace for the leisurely flow that was vintage Mystic Ridge.

Angel closed her eyes and let the swing sway in weightless motion. The spicy fragrant air, the people—this was Mystic Ridge. It felt good to be home.

The scent of man and musk greeted her and her stomach jumped at the familiarity. He was here. Finally.

Two hands slid up her shoulders, nudged and sent the swing into a gentle rhythm. Excitement curled through her veins and raced toward her head.

"Welcome home."

Peter's deep voice caressed her and warmed the cool breeze.

"Peter Richland." Angel wished she hadn't whispered his name so softly. She sounded as if she had been waiting for him. "What a surprise."

He stopped the swing, and came around.

Unable to find the strength to stand, Angel pushed back on her heels and looked up. So he'd known where she'd been all along. Her roiling emotions vacillated between flattery and disappointment. Why hadn't he come around sooner?

"They teach you that in California?" Again the deep texture of his voice rolled over her like warm butter on a hot roll.

"What?"

"To lie to old friends."

An argument as dusty and old as the ground beneath her feet resurfaced and Angel wondered where Peter was going. Surely he'd gotten over her leaving Mystic Ridge for a better life. "Don't be ridiculous." To establish more even footing, she found her professional voice. "How are you, Peter?"

He gazed into her eyes, his expression serious. "How do I look?"

"Healthy. Strong." Sexy. "Good."

He stooped his tall frame down in front of her. "What was that glint in your eyes before you said good?"

Angel averted her gaze so the truth wouldn't spill from her lips. "Nothing."

"You were never shy, Angelina. You always spoke your mind. Every thought. Every idea. Always the truth." His voice dipped low. "Is lying an institution on the West Coast or can you buy a video and learn like that Tae-bo?" She must have looked surprised because he said, "We do get cable in these parts."

Angel laughed at herself, at him. "Of course not." He was pushing to know who she was, searching to see if there was any resemblance to the woman who'd left so long ago. She wanted to say she was the same, but held back. Peter had no right to be so familiar with her. Other men had tried and failed. And as much as Peter tried to regain ground, she resisted.

Only his voice stroked her, filled her up with seductive memories of the past and romanticized their youth. Her body fairly hummed and all she could imagine was for him to hold her and never let her go.

The thought scared her.

That thought was a 'marry me' thought. And Angel would never do that. The path was littered with men who'd asked and been rejected.

California was scarce on men who sought the truth. Between the ego-fragile actors, the wannabes, the men who shunned "the business" and the boys from the valley, few had ever wanted to keep it real.

But Peter was real. His denim shirt hugged a six pack of muscles that her hands itched to remember. Long legs were tucked into worn jeans, his feet pressed into broken-in boots.

On his head he wore a newer version of the high school's baseball cap, and where he once wore glasses, dark brown orbs looked clear into her. His hands teetered inches from her waist and his mouth—Angel recalled how it felt to the touch.

"Tell me." He spoke slowly. "Your thought between strong and good."

He still hadn't touched her and she yearned for it. "Are you married, Peter?" In her heart she prayed she wouldn't crumble to pieces with his answer.

"No." Emphatic. Direct. The same Peter.

His finger touched her breastbone. Angel stood as if under the influence of a powerful magnet. The swing's linked chain lined her spine and she answered him. "Sexy."

He answered with a pleased chuckle that made her day.

Peter moved to embrace her.

Angel felt his power, his strength, the safety he offered and let herself lean into him. Her body shook as she vowed to hug him and let him go, because she knew what touching him would do. Remind her of the last time he'd held her. Been over her. Inside her. Beneath her.

His arms glided slowly around her back and he seemed to lift her off her feet as he brought her closer. They hovered, until she felt the muscles in his arms contract.

Angel closed her eyes.

And he squeezed.

A thousand points of light burst in her head. In her heart she commanded time to stand still. The moans of the cattle in the distant fields ceased and the insects hushed.

Angel listened to Peter's strong, steady heartbeat and felt hers slow to meet the pace. They stayed this way for what seemed an eternity.

"Welcome home, Angelina."

"Thank you. Call me Angel."

Like a stalled carousel infused with a jolt of electricity, reality lurched into their world. One by one, the sounds of bugs, animals, music from the house and voices filtered through the haze of their reunion.

Peter stepped back as if he just remembered an important obligation. His eyes held a distant curiosity and his arms fell to his side. "Angel? When did that happen?"

Wary of his reaction to her new self, Angel clasped her hands together and stepped back. "It's just one of those things. Angelina can be such a mouthful."

"No one around here ever had a problem with it."

So this was it. Her leaving would stand between them. She'd come back stronger, and more confident than the person that had left, but obviously Peter couldn't handle it.

"I'm still me."

His gaze took in the mass of ringlet curls, her designer clothes and the choker around her neck and Angel could just imagine his thoughts.

He nodded as if in acquiescence. "So, what brings you home?"

Careful, she warned herself. Peter was a man who needed time to adjust to change. Angel could tell that from the way he looked at her. She pushed a curl behind her ear.

"I came home to see my mom and Luther." They took leisurely steps back toward the house. Now that wasn't a lie. "And do a bit of business in Maryland."

"Ah," he nodded. His voice slid into the night. "How long are you staying?"

Their eyes met. A hundred unspoken questions filled the space between them, but Angel couldn't bring herself to move away. It felt good to be in his presence and she answered as truthfully as she could. "Until my work is done."

"So you just came home to take care of some business and see your folks. Nothing to rush back to?"

"I beg your pardon?"

He shrugged. "You might have a dog or a cat or a tiger." Angel started to laugh. "I don't know," he said. "Or you might have somebody."

She pulled her top lip between her teeth and mois-
tened her lips. "No tigers allowed in my county. I
don't have dogs or," she hesitated and watched him
draw in a deep breath. She smiled slowly. "Cats."

Their right feet hit the bottom stair at the same
time. "If I didn't know better, Peter Richland, I'd
think you wanted to know if I were involved."

Angel put her hand on the beveled white post and
swung to face him. "What I can't imagine is why that
would be of interest to you."

"A man can't satisfy his curiosity?"

"Most definitely." She leaned against the post,
curious about him, too. How had he managed to stay
single? Why hadn't life changed him? Why had he
stayed in Mystic Ridge?

She knew that his job as the town council president held the prestige afforded to the Mayor of a
larger city.

Peter made the decisions here and his opinion was
sought after and well-respected. She knew in order to
bring a company the size of a Mall-mart into the area,
she'd have to go through him, but she wanted to get a
feel for the town and the people on her own. The time
would come when they would sit across from each
other in a boardroom, but tonight they might as well
have been eighteen again. Keep it light, she told
herself.

Angel crossed her arms and answered him. "Well,
old friend, I'm single. So—"

He pulled her by her crossed arms until his mouth was inches from hers. "Well then, old friend. Let me give you a proper welcome home."

Peter's mouth covered hers in a sensual meeting that sent a bolt of pleasure rocketing through her.

In an instant of blind pleasure, she opened her mouth...and met cool air.

He was gone.

Angel opened her eyes. The bright light from the porch blinded her briefly. Her chin fell to her chest. It was just a friendly kiss. Embarrassed, she covered her mouth and dried her lips.

"Coming in?" Peter said.

Angel couldn't meet his gaze as she stepped past him and walked into the house. "You'll pay for that— old friend," she said under her breath as her relatives greeted him with raucous hellos.

They accepted beers from her cousin. Then Peter slid his index finger down her shoulder blade.

Angel pivoted, knowing his touch anywhere. He tapped his can with hers. "Looking forward to it."

CHAPTER FOUR

Dahia whooped and tossed Sheba into the air. They hugged like sisters, then realized what they were doing and snapped apart. Sheba shifted the fabric around her legs and shoved her chin into the air. "You're insane. I do not know what has come over you."

Dahia danced by, her eyes glittering like African gold. "Our job is done. They have kissed. Now I can receive the final crown."

Nefertiti shot Sheba a warning glance, and Dahia's eyes turned into a sparkling obsidian. "Queen Dahia," Nefertiti said. The woman whirled around, her spine ramrod straight. "Look at the lifeline on your palm. Is it not faint like mine? Like Sheba's?"

"It is not!" she declared, staring at her hand. She closed it into a tight fist. "Mine is dark like the earth's richest soil."

"Mine, too, is dark," Sheba said. Surprised, Nefertiti stood, looked into Dahia's then Sheba's extended hand.

Dahlia's hand looked as if the bark of an oak had been etched into it. Sheba's was more the color of clay.

Nefertiti unfurled her fingers and stared at her palm. The color of sand.

"Look, sisters," she exclaimed, excited. "We are making a difference. It is working."

"Working? It is done. We are done. Are we not?" Dahia said, suddenly unsure.

Sheba examined their palms and touched the center. "Storm clouds are rising. Dahia, you are the warrior priestess. Angelina is approaching her fiercest battle. Will she survive?"

The priestess was able to view flashes of peril ahead. "She will be wounded," she said gravely. "But she will survive."

They turned to view Angel as she walked through town, reacquainting herself with the people. After acquiring two parcels of land from gentlemen at the retirement home, she stopped at the daycare and spoke to the elderly. Soaked up their wisdom, shared her youth.

As the day shifted towards afternoon, her steps slowed, her shoulders heavy, her thoughts jumbled. She'd learned much about Mystic Ridge, her home-town. It was the same, yet different.

The queens felt the draw on her strength.

Without words they linked arms, stood shoulder to shoulder and infused their energy into Angel.

As her stride ate up the wooden sidewalks, her head arched toward the sun. "She can feel us. Go forth and conquer, priestess," Dahia said strongly.

Angel jogged toward her car, confidence replacing her worry.

Nefertiti clapped her hands and smiled.

～

Peter sat across from Roy Cochran, the only real estate agent within four counties, and tried to look interested while Roy expounded on the health of his livestock.

But Peter's eyes kept closing and each time they did, he saw Angelina. Beautiful, sexy Angelina. Desire heated his blood to a simmer and made him adjust, not for the first time, in his seat.

Roy misinterpreted the movement and hurried along. "I know you're a busy man, but the reason I stopped by was to tell you that somebody has bought up about seventy-five acres of land that comprise the south bank."

Surprised, Peter sat up. The land known as the south bank represented Mystic Ridge's beginning. It had been built by runaway and freed slaves four hundred years ago.

By way of compensation, each of the original families in Mystic Ridge owned five acres of the south bank and had agreed to never sell the land so that it would be a legacy for future generations. The fact that strangers owned it alarmed him.

"How much did you say is gone?"

"About seventy-five of the three hundred acres." Roy sat forward. "Joe and Lacy Jordan called and mentioned that some surveyors from Baltimore stopped by the truck stop and said they were working on some land called the south bank. Lacy got right on the phone and called me and I came by to see you."

Peter nodded his appreciation. "You did the right thing. But if you didn't handle the deals, how is it gone?"

Roy scratched his grizzly whiskers with thick fingers.

"Apparently somebody has been paying the taxes on land that was forgotten about when some of the old folks died. Recently the papers were filed in Baltimore and the property converted to a company's name." He dug into his breast pocket. "The Dyer Corporation."

Peter scratched down the ominous sounding name. Big companies were always trying to encroach upon the tranquility of Mystic Ridge. Years ago it had been condo developers and before that homey B&B's.

It seems hardworking city folk needed a place to rest on the weekend and with Mystic Ridge being four hours between two major cities, many thought it a perfect place to escape—with a few minor improvements.

Most of Mystic Ridge's citizens liked the tourism dollars, but they wanted people to enjoy Mystic Ridge just as it was. Peter cringed every time he thought of what had become of Savannah, Georgia. That land had once been home to settlers and now was one of the biggest tourist attractions in Georgia. Only it wasn't the native Blacks that were rich. They'd sold land to developers dirt cheap and now worked on land they once owned.

Seventy-five acres of the south bank was significant. He tried not to convey his alarm and opted for damage control.

"Roy, are the purchased sections connected?"

The older man shook his head. "But there's a possibility that they could be. Lula Mae Clay owns one piece, your daddy owns another and about five separate pieces are owned by some of the old folks in Tracey's Retirement Home. All told, they need about seven more pieces to connect what they've got."

"That's good news. Whoever is buying can be stopped. They seem to have gotten the easiest lots first. But the rest of us won't sell." Peter grabbed his baseball cap and he and Roy shrugged into winter jackets.

Brenda had already gone to lunch and Peter didn't expect her back for another hour. He decided to take his daily walk and figure out how to handle this latest development.

His breath huffed in front of him and he slowed his stride to accommodate Roy's slower pace. "Peter, would it be so bad for a business to come in?"

"Not if it were the right one."

"What's right in your mind?"

Peter shook his head. "My preference is for Mystic Ridge to remain a small town where the people know their neighbors and look out for one another. Towns

like ours that grow too fast, invite trouble. We don't
have the resources to fight drugs and crime. We don't
have to worry about locking our doors, and if we
forget, we're not worried.

"Our town has the lowest divorce rate in the state
because we know the meaning of family. I won't jeop-
ardize all that we've built. Believe me, Roy, Mystic
Ridge is fine just the way it is."

When Roy continued his silent contemplation,
Peter pressed on. "Do you want pollution and crime
to invade your life?" Peter urged Roy to look at the
mountains. "Do you want all this to disappear? The
peace? The hominess? That's what would happen.
Trust me," he said, determined to make his longtime
family friend understand. "You don't want that."

Roy hooked his hands together behind his back.
"No, I don't. But my son and daughter-in-law can't
stay in Mystic Ridge without having jobs that will
support the life they deserve. They've got degrees in
marketing. What can they do here?"

Aware of the flat economy and lack of jobs, Peter
nodded his head in agreement. "True, Mystic Ridge
isn't Baltimore or D.C., but I promise you, whatever
company is buying up that much land will destroy
this town. I can't let that happen. I'll do some research
on them today and by this evening I should have a
clear picture of what they want."

They stopped in front of Roy's office and the man's
eyes were sad. His gaze roamed over the cream stucco
building before meeting Peter's.

"Junior and Sharon are all Muriel and I have left. If they leave, we're going with them. I don't know too many of us old folks who don't want to be around their grand kids. If a company is interested, we should listen. Think about it, Peter."

Roy clapped him on the shoulder and Peter considered his words as he stopped at Bunny's hair salon. He greeted the ladies, ranging in age from eighteen to eighty, and guided them into a conversation about the economy. The spirited conversation gave him insight to everyone's feelings, but the consensus was that they were satisfied with Mystic Ridge's present state.

After a brief stop at the daycare and the Apothecary, Peter continued on his stroll to Clay's General store. Maureen stepped from the aisles and greeted him with a big smile. "Peter. Good to see you."

"Thanks, Maureen." He removed his hat. "Miss Lula Mae up?"

"No, she's down for a nap with little Will. I think she sleeps longer than he does most days. Anything I can do for you?"

After listening to the ladies at the salon, Peter didn't want to start a four-alarm talk-fest about the south bank, so he backed toward the door, "Thanks, but no. I'll see Miss Lula Mae tomorrow."

"All right then."

He stepped outside, when struck with a thought. "Can I borrow your phone, Maureen?" ·

She walked behind the register and handed him the cordless. "Help yourself. I'm running to the back for a second. Just leave it on the counter when you're done."

Peter dialed Lacy at the truck stop. When he finished, he hung up and strode back to his office and hopped into his truck.

It seems that someone other than the surveyors were interested in the grassy lands that made up the south bank.

Lacy had just given Angelina Snowden a large cup of coffee and short cut directions.

CHAPTER FIVE

Angel stepped from her car and drank in the sight of the lush fields that spanned for miles, rich and vibrant under the native sun.

Birds cawed overhead, dipping and swirling in the magnificent daylight. She shielded her eyes with her hand and executed a deliberate three-hundred-sixty-degree turn.

Everywhere she looked, she noticed pearls of the earth's beauty. A duck tucked his neck and dove in for a landing. A raccoon scuttled along the bank of trees. A family of deer darted into the brush.

The south bank had changed in fifteen years. When she had last visited, cars could proceed only so far on the gravel roads. Now paved roads led the way and as she followed the precise directions through unfamiliar woods, she heard the lap of water. Nostalgia stole over her.

Peter brought her here once to Point Royal Lake. Just thinking of him gave rise to guilty feelings. He deserved to know the real reason why she'd come home.

She strolled the edge of the body of water, reacquainting herself, then stooped and gathered a handful of pebbles. One at a time, she tossed them into the lake, each ripple finding its way back to her.

You are the pebble and all that you do will touch others, and you will be blessed.

It was the same voice from the car, only Angel wasn't afraid. A strong sense of responsibility overcame her and she wrapped her arms around herself and twisted in the cool breeze. If she ever questioned why she'd come home, she had her answer. Mystic Ridge needed her. Just as she needed to connect with the people she and Peter once were.

When they'd come to Point Royal, they'd been full of youthful ideals. They'd planned a future at this lake and she smiled as she remembered their brazen thirst for life.

But the very ideas that brought them together had torn them apart. Peter wouldn't consider making a life outside of Mystic Ridge. And she couldn't reconcile that Mystic Ridge was the only choice for life.

Dreams had pushed her to leave and saw her through six years of UC Berkeley. Master's degree in hand, she'd paved her way in the world until she was at this lakeside—right back home.

Angel shook her head.

Behind her trees rustled, and she turned in time to see Peter burst through a patch of dense foliage. Surprised, her heartbeat increased and she fought off a welcoming smile. He deserved to know the truth. She couldn't deny him that.

His arms were laden with a patchwork quilt and a thermos.

Glory, he looked handsome. Taller than the average man, he couldn't help but grab attention. Crayola brown, with a serious face he'd earned from his daddy, he squinted at the eastern sun and adjusted his baseball cap.

He took his time joining her and Angel felt herself waiting for him to grace her with a word. "Angelina."

Uh-oh. "Peter Dawson Homer Richland."

His head whipped sideways. "Don't call me that. You know I hate that name."

"Call me Angel." He looked as if he would protest. "A compromise works best if both parties agree."

Angel kicked at some rocks and closed her eyes on a burst of cool air. "How did you know I was here?"

"Mystic is small. Lacy told me. The temperature is changing and here you are in the woods, at the lake, in high heels, unprepared," he scolded.

"Aw. You care."

He shrugged off her sarcasm.

"Joke if you want, but I'll bet you couldn't find your way back to your car if I laid a hundred dollars in your hand."

She accepted the challenge and pointed in one direction, turned, and pointed over her shoulder. Suddenly the woods all looked alike. "Well…I'd have found it eventually."

"If the bears didn't find you first."

She gave him a disbelieving look. "I don't scare that easily." To prove her point, she let him walk a few yards away before she followed and sat on the blankets he'd laid down. Angel took a grateful sip of hot coffee.

Resting his elbow on his propped up knee, he pulled blades of grass from the ground, tore them into strands and pointed straight ahead.

At the far end of the lake, two deer broke from the forest, sipped water then abruptly lifted their heads to view them. Angel felt the scrutiny from all the locals. The deer turned and ran. Peter stayed and gave her a look she couldn't avoid any longer.

"Mystic Ridge," he began, "is Maryland's mistress. She's the best kept, most seductive secret the state has ever had."

"Secrets are almost always revealed."

He shook his head. "The beauty of our town is that we're forgettable. For four hundred years we've managed to keep out people who want to hurt us. Change us. Strip the innocence under the guise of 'helping us advance.' Shame, isn't it?"

She felt as if she'd been punched in the stomach. "What," she whispered.

"That outsiders, people who haven't ever loved this town the way I love it, think they know what's best."

Angel thought of all the small town jokes she'd fielded in L.A. because of her accent. How during her first years at Berkeley she'd worked hard to smooth it out, make it twang less. How over time, she'd become less the butt of jokes, and more the perpetrator.

"I love it, too, Peter," she said, but felt the words fall from her mouth and shatter like panes of glass. Had she really changed? When had her resentment for the livestock, and dirt, and one stoplight town turned to love? Confused, Angel didn't know.

And until she knew, she couldn't perpetuate a falsehood. She'd already lied enough. Tonight when he came to her step-father's meeting, he'd know why she was home. The whole town would and from then on things would be different.

Deep in her own thoughts, she was startled when she felt Peter behind her. His long legs snuggled up beside hers and he embraced her. Warmth emanated from him and penetrated through her back. "I'm glad to hear that. Maybe you'll find lots of reasons to stay."

Even as wanting rocked her system, she couldn't give in. Stay? Staying in Mystic Ridge would mean abandoning all she'd worked for. No matter how much she wanted to share Peter's warmth, she could only pray that when it was time for her to go, there wouldn't be any emotional hang-ups.

"The last time we were here was pretty special," he said.

"That's because you thought you were getting some," she reminded him.

"And I didn't?"

Her cheeks grew hot. She closed her eyes, glad he couldn't see her face. "You tried," she conceded.

"Tried, hmm. Let me test my thirty-two-year-old memory."

His hands slipped beneath her wool jacket and found the softness of her poplin shirt. They moved in gentle strokes across her belly, settling her back against him.

Low and easy, he started to speak. "We came up here one August night, the heat hanging thick in the air. I laid down one of Ruth's soft patchwork quilts and lowered you beside me. You looked so expectant and shy and I felt your innocence. I knew the night was special for us and I wanted to give you the very best I could."

She rocked gently on the cadence of his voice. She felt the heat now, remembered it from way back when.

"You wore the prettiest pink top with these tiny pearl buttons and I took my time releasing each one. I needed to see you. Had to. You were beautiful." His lips touched her behind her ear. "You're more beautiful now. With each button, I saw your skin, wanted to touch it. Feel its softness beneath my fingertips. Like now."

"Yes."

He pulled the long zipper that started at the neck, and in a lazy motion, opened her to his exploration.

He didn't reach for her breasts although they strained for his touch. His fingers found her neck, tipped her head to lean on his shoulder. Angel released the last of her reserve and rested against him.

"Your bra was stark white against your skin and I pulled it down one shoulder and up on the other." His laughter was full of anything but humor. "Didn't know what I was doing. Just wanted to touch you."

Her bra snapped open on her back.

"Figured out finesse, I see," she sighed.

His large hands covered the slopes, her nipple caught between his middle and ring finger. The pressure was enough to make her moan aloud. "It was worth it to feel you like this."

They stayed this way, him stroking her breasts, making her hot in the confines of the old quilt.

Touching her breasts was safe. But she wanted to hear the rest. "Tell me, Peter."

"I couldn't stop with just touching your breasts, tasting them. I had to know your hidden treasures." His hand touched her belly. Searched lower. "You had on these blue shorts with this ruffle around the legs. Never seen anything sexier than that in my young life."

"Really," she said, feeling his hand snake slowly towards her center. Her breathing shallowed. She anticipated. Hoped. Prayed.

He touched.

Her heart sang.

"The shorts were gone and the white panties disappeared. There you were. Naked before me. I wanted to see pleasure in your eyes." His hand cupped her at the apex of her body and she pushed into his chest and lifted her hips. Through her panties his thumb played her like she were the string on a precious violin. Her body had its own music and it felt sweet with Peter as its maestro.

"I laid you down and went on a search to find every curve, bend and fold that would bring you pleasure. Make you feel good, special."

She pulled air deep into her lungs. Teetering on the edge. If only…he would let her go over.

Needing to, she lifted her hips and for a second she was airborne.

Then lying beneath him.

His breath touched her cheeks, her lips. "I want you." The length of him pressed into her and she moved not to tease, but to satisfy. "No protection."

"Next time," he said, lifting her butt into his hands and rocking himself against her until the bright blue sky shattered into a million drops of silver stars.

His coat was still on. Hers gaped open.

Her body tingled in the wind.

His manhood stood prominent against his jeans. "Peter," she whispered. Her body trembled.

"You said my name just like that the last time." He caught the tip of her nose between his teeth.

Angel closed her eyes. He'd see the truth. Truth and betrayal couldn't co-exist. "You're embarrassing me."

"Don't be. It's just me. Peter."

His mouth descended toward hers. Discouraging him was an option, but anticipation rose and Angel couldn't fight it. She wanted his kiss as much as she wanted her next breath.

His gaze flicked over her. Then his mouth covered hers, knowing the valleys and plains, staking chartered territory. His tongue lined her lips and she parted, tasting him with fervor and longing.

Shudders of pleasure zinged through her and Angel sank deeper into his kiss. But guilt sneaked in. Stole the joy, tarnished the passion and usurped her desire.

Sadness rushed in and her mouth slid from his. She buried her face in his collar. She was using him. Misleading him.

He must have sensed her emotional withdrawal. "Don't ever tell me you're sorry this happened. We're not children. I want you. All the way. Remember that." He pushed to his feet and the cold rushed in and enveloped her. He gave her a hand up. "One day at a time."

"Right."

"We'd better get back. I've still got a couple of hours work to finish."

Work. Yes. The reason why I'm home in the first place. "I do, too."

He helped her rearrange her clothes, gathered the blanket and she the coffee.

Angel followed him through the woods, glad to concentrate on the rough terrain.

Ten minutes later, she slid into her car. "Thank you for," she searched for the right words, "coming to see me."

He leaned on the door and kissed her hard. As a reminder.

Then he stepped back. Looked directly into her eyes. "Would you know anything about surveyors up in these parts?"

Her heart raced so fast, she became lightheaded. What had Dyer done? No surveyors were supposed to be up here until the last parcel of land was secured. Had they gone behind her back? No, they trusted her to do her job. Perhaps one of the families wanted to get their property staked.

She shook her head and squeezed her eyes shut in a silent prayer.

"What's the matter?" he said.

"I-I haven't eaten."

"See you later?" His eyes conveyed interest and longing.

"I have a thing tonight at my parents home."

Peter nodded. "L.A. talk is interesting. A thing." He shrugged, his grin seducing her sinning soul. "Luther invited me over, too. I'll see you there." He caressed the car's bright red finish. "And maybe afterwards."

Her breath caught in her throat. "Yeah. Maybe."

"Follow me. I want to make sure you and your fancy car make it back safely."

His truck rumbled to life and she trailed him back to Mystic Ridge. He cast a hearty wave when she veered right at the fork leading to her mother's house.

How deceitful have I become? Has L.A. turned me into a pathological liar, or do I lie for sport?

Grateful her mother was gone, Angel climbed into a hot bath, but couldn't soak away the guilt of knowing how hurt Peter would be later tonight.

CHAPTER SIX

The engine on Peter's truck sputtered and the car shut down. Steering to the dusty shoulder, he turned the key. *Click.* The battery was dead.

He got out on the road, figuring the distance to Luther and Ruth's house, and completed the mile trek in just under fifteen minutes.

Angel's car was parked on the grass some distance from the house, leaving room for all the familiar vehicles. Looked like the whole town council was there.

Pushing the handle on the front door, he let himself in and was greeted with friendly hellos.

Ruth came and hooked arms with him. "I didn't hear you pull up."

"My battery died a mile up the road." He grinned down at her. "You sure have perked up since Angelina—Angel got home."

"She gives me a reason to smile."

"Looks good on you. Where's everybody?"

"Out back. I'll take you. It's not often I get to hold hands with a handsome young man."

"Ruth," he chided with a big smile. "You're making me blush."

The familiar rooms teemed with life and he felt a sense of peacefulness. He would always remember coming to the Snowden's house. The couple used to host lavish parties for employees of the Snowden Glass Company, one of the town's largest employers.

As a summer intern, he'd reported directly to Luther and learned the finer points of leadership and balancing good business sense with politics.

Many nights he'd eaten at their table and sat on their porch. And under a full moon, he'd romanced their daughter and fallen in love.

The Snowdens had been good for Mystic Ridge. It pleased him to see the family together again.

Peter kept an eye out for Angelina, but didn't see her. "Looks like you have a house full. What's going on?"

"You know Luther. Always has—"

"Something to say," they finished together and laughed.

Ruth patted his hand and guided him toward the back porch where the men had gathered. "Why don't you go on out. I'll get you something cold to drink."

He wanted to ask her why her smile seemed forced, but instead stepped onto the deck where men smoked cigars, lounged in wooden rocking chairs, sharing laughter and the fading sun.

The smell of grilled food reminded him that he'd missed dinner, but he'd grab a plate later.

He headed toward his father who stood in the corner talking to Luther, and accepted the cold beer from Ruth. "Dad, I didn't know you'd be here."

"I got to get out sometimes."

"You're on the lake eighteen hours a day. That's not out enough?"

His father, Peter Sr., looked at Luther. "This boy thinks he knows everything."

Fondness radiated from Luther's eyes. "He ought to. We trust our town in his hands."

"That we do."

Feminine laughter made the trio turn. Angel had approached from behind and Peter stepped aside to give her room. He'd taken a swallow of beer and felt it go down as slow as it took for his eyes to take her all in.

Her long legs were clad in dark tights that ended in a beige skirt. A beaded belt hung from the waist and he resisted the urge to tug it. A long-sleeved pristine white T-shirt nestled her chest, covered slightly by a black quilted vest. "You do what?" Angel asked.

Luther pressed his lips to Angelina's forehead. "We trust Peter with our town."

Her head dipped and she nodded, a strained smile on her lips. She was worried, Peter knew intuitively, pleased that he could still read more than one of her emotions after all this time.

"How does everything look to you, Angel?"

She hesitated and Peter stiffened, wanting her to love Mystic Ridge or at least not tear it down.

"Everything looks…smaller. I feel like I've grown taller in a doll house." She angled to look at him, holding back curls. "I didn't realize how good it would feel to be with family and friends." Her eyes never left Peter's.

"Well, we're glad you're back, too," Luther said. "We'd better get started. The night promises to be long."

When Luther disappeared into the house, Peter gave Angelina his full attention. "Any idea what he's talking about?" A distinct feeling of discomfort stole over him when she waved a hand in front of her.

"You know Luther. He doesn't like to have his light stolen. Let's just hang out until he's ready."

The suggestion conjured up so many images, Peter couldn't help leaning close to her. A soft citrus scent floated on a breeze toward him as she leaned on the railing, overlooking rolling pastures. "I meant what I said, Peter. It's good to be back home."

"Are you ready to tell me what brought you back?"

"I came home to help—"

Luther's voice cut her off. "Will everyone come inside? It's time to get started."

Angel's eyes filled with a mixture of hope and reserve. She had clasped her hands together and Peter took one in his. She looked down at his fingers pressed to her palm. "I want to see you afterwards."

"Peter, I don't know."

"I know."

Concession lit the dark orbs behind the yellow shades. "Okay, we'll talk."

The men brought in chairs so everyone could sit together in the living room. About fifteen of Mystic Ridge's influential families were present as well as council members and neighbors.

Peter settled down on the overstuffed sofa and made room for Angel, but she stood by her mother in the doorway just behind Luther's shoulder.

"Friends," Luther began. "I asked you to come here today because what I do will affect you. I came to this town twenty-two years ago and fell in love. With the town, and especially the people. I met a beautiful woman who stole my heart. We got married and I opened my family's Irish glass-making business, and as they say, the rest is history.

"Our life wasn't always easy. We took a lot of heat being an interracial couple, but we made it. She stood by me during the tough years and now it's time for me to give her my undivided attention. I'm stepping down from the helm of Snowden Glass and—" he looked down, suddenly emotional "—closing its doors."

A shock wave hit Peter with the force of a lightning bolt. How would the town survive? Snowden Glass was one of the biggest employers.

Why hadn't Angel mentioned Luther's retirement this afternoon? She'd seemed distracted, but he'd chalked it up to her being in the woods with her ex-boyfriend who was doing his best to make a move on her. Instead of taking care of town business and knowing this was about to occur, his mind and body had been preoccupied. Anger and disappointment shot through him.

"Why do you have to close down?" Bunny asked. "Can't you get another president?"

"We aren't competitive anymore. The younger companies are doing things better and faster. Most of their business outside of manufacturing is web based. Unfortunately, the problem is two-fold. We aren't competitive and the cost of doing business from current resources is prohibitive."

Maureen Clay spoke up. "We do great with the specialty bottles. Can't you keep that division open?"

"It's a matter of supply and demand. We just don't get enough orders."

"How soon?" she asked.

"Two months."

Suddenly, everyone started to talk at once. "What are we going to do?"

"We'll have to move."

"Give up my land," snorted Jesse Transom, great grandson to one of Mystic Ridge's first settlement families. "No way. I was here before Mr. Moneybags showed up and I'll be here after."

"Peter?"

"Peter?"

The sound of his name filled his head and Peter wished he'd worn his glasses. At least he'd have something to do with his hands. He dragged his gaze away from Angelina and started to stand, when she spoke up.

"I'd like to throw something out." Everyone sensed the tension. Felt his anger mingle with theirs. They hushed. "If you don't mind."

"What is it, Angelina?" Peter's father said.

She looked directly at Peter. "I mighty be able to offer a solution."

He lowered himself to his seat. "You have a captive audience."

Her voice shook but grew stronger as she talked.

"I know how much Snowden Glass has meant to Mystic Ridge. I've watched my step-father and my mother dedicate their lives to making it a success. I didn't know before I returned home that this was going to happen, but where there is an ending, there is a beginning. The company I work for loves to do business with small towns."

Interested eyes turned Angelina's way and the weight of anger dissipated into a desperate-like fungus. Panicked eyes darted between them.

"Who is this and where do we sign up," said Bunny. Invisible red flags flew up, but Peter chose to pick his moment. "What company is this?"

"The Dyer Corporation," Angel said calmly. "They build shopping complexes."

The women in the group whispered excitedly. But Peter zeroed in on what she wasn't saying. "Shopping complexes," he said ruefully. "I seem to recall reading somewhere—" Angel tried to cut him off, but Peter wouldn't be railroaded. "Dyer owns—"

"Mall-Mart," they said in unison.

Peter spoke as if they were the only two in the room. "Dyer is the company that bought up land in the south bank. This morning surveyors went out and marked their land from ours."

He now had everyone's attention. Ray Cochran hung his head while Maureen Clay's and Bunny's mouth gaped. Everyone else sat in stony silence.

"Congratulations. Someone has just put a price on our heritage. Is that what you want?" One by one, heads shook.

"Sorry, Angel. No deal. Mystic Ridge isn't for sale."

CHAPTER SEVEN

Peter's proclamation jabbed a hole in her carefully planned proposal and deflated Angel's enthusiasm. His words were filled with hurt, anger and resolve.

He'd go to his grave trying to protect the town and the people who entrusted their well-being in his hands. Instead of being angry about his opposition, Angel reached out to him.

"You're right. Mystic Ridge isn't for sale."

"What?" he cried in disbelief. "You're agreeing with me?"

"Yes." Glances volleyed between them.

He laughed, one hand on his hip, the other stroking his upper lip. "Why do I smell a dead fish?"

"Come on now, son. She said you were right. You don't have to treat Angelina this way."

She briefly met Peter Sr.'s gaze then returned to look at his son. She read not only disbelief, but distrust. Guilt gripped her. "No, Mr. Richland. Peter is entitled to his opinion. I agree Mystic Ridge isn't for sale, but this town needs a business so that we don't go under. I have a company that's interested in making this town successful."

"We?" Peter said. "You're back home for the first time in fifteen years and you expect us to believe that you have our best interest at heart?"

"I can see why some of you might have reservations." A growing murmur began to swell. "But i believe you said the operative word. Home. Mystic Ridge will always be my home. I want to see it survive."

"By selling off pieces of sacred land," Jesse Transom said matter-of-factly. He rose, leaning heavily on his cane and headed for the door. "That land has been ours since the first slaves walked out of the south. I won't stand by and let it be desecrated by strangers."

Several of the older folks followed him out the door. The rest looked scared.

Roy Cochran leaned forward, elbows on his knees. "Don't let them bother you," he reassured. "They're old and don't want change to leave them behind." He smoothed his salt and pepper hair. "I don't either. But the fact remains if this hadn't happened now, it would have happened later. My son and daughter-in-law can't find jobs around here. If Muriel and I pack up and go with them, what does the south bank mean to me?"

Angel hated the position Dyer had put her in. They'd compromised the delicate balance of this mission and were not allowing her to do her job. The support several locals gave fueled her desire to see this deal through to fruition. Roy gave her a thumbs up and Angel grasped at his overture. "Thank you for the vote of confidence."

Peter quickly jumped in. "No disrespect intended," he said to Luther, "but this town was surviving before Snowden Glass. We can again, if necessary."

"Now, Peter are you saying you won't even consider hearing a proposal by Dyer?" Bunny said.

Stormy eyes glanced around as he struggled for the right words. "I would consider it if they'd approached us in the right way. Buying land from under our noses is underhanded. There's no telling what else will happen. We have two months. I don't see why we can't look into various opportunities instead of immediately jumping into the first one that comes our way."

"I agree," Angel said, "but this is a great opportunity and I'd hate to see Mystic Ridge lose out."

Their gazes penetrated Angel and she felt as if she were in a room full of hot air.

"You agree," Peter reiterated.

"Yes. I can straighten out the land situation and give you as much information as you need. I have charts and facts and demographics, facts from other cities this size and later this week I should receive a detailed analysis from their local officials."

Maureen stood and gathered her purse. "Peter, I think you should review all the information before you dismiss this out of hand. As a member of the town council, I vote that you two work together and present us with a proposal."

Peter's father stood, as did other council members. "All in favor of Peter and Angel working this into something we can understand say 'aye.'"

"Ayes" resounded.

"Opposed?" He waited a second. "The 'Ayes' have it."

A slow procession filed between them, Peter on one side and Angel on the other.

Relieved the idea hadn't been shot down completely, Angel wondered if working so closely with Peter was the best course of action. Although he probably hated her now and would find her betrayal unforgivable, ever since she had seen him, they could hardly keep their hands off each other.

She stepped aside as her parents accepted hugs and quiet congratulations until finally, the house was quiet.

Luther studied the couple and grabbed his wife's hand.

"Ruth, let's go out back and see the—trees."

Her mother laughed as she walked with her husband. "Honey, just say you want to be alone with me..."

Their voices faded and Angel turned to Peter. His face was taut, his eyes narrowed. His mouth had turned upside down and anger drifted off him in waves.

"What was this afternoon about?" he demanded.

She'd asked herself that very question a thousand times but couldn't form a coherent answer. An unknown force seemed to have taken hold of her emotions and wrapped them around Peter. She'd thought of nothing else all day.

"Did you come home thinking you could romance your high school sweetheart into getting what you wanted?"

Angel shook her head, speechless. She should have known this would hurt. That he'd think this way. In fact, she felt the opposite of manipulative. They shared a unique harmony that couldn't be described with words. She felt it now, even as his anger invaded every cell in her body.

This couldn't be love, she thought as her skin prickled and her stomach jumped. Love wasn't supposed to hurt this deep and make her want to fall over herself apologizing.

Angel opened her mouth to speak and he stepped forward expectant. "What, then, Angelina?" His bark of laughter tore at her heart. "I know how you see me now. I'm just a country boy living in a backwards, one-horse town who never made it out of the boon-docks." He shrugged his acceptance. "But I love this town and I'll protect it from everyone," his voice lowered. "Even you. Go back to California. You're not one of us anymore."

Peter started for the door, the bright overhead light stark against his retreating back. She didn't want him to go. Didn't want him to leave on these terms. This afternoon had been special. But she had a job to do. And so did he.

She spoke up, her voice displaying none of her inner struggle. "I'm not leaving, so get that out of your head. If you take your job so seriously, why aren't you listening to what your constituents have to say? You remember the other twenty-five thousand or so people with Mystic Ridge on their birth certificates, including me. You can't make me or invite me or tell me to leave. I have a job to do."

"So do I."

At a loss, she shook her head saying, "Did you invent the saying 'My way or the highway'?"

His hand stopped on the door. He stood between the frame and freedom and gazed at her. "You don't get it, do you?"

Angel planted her hands on her hips. "I get it, all right. I get the fact that you're running from change. You're giving people a false sense of security if you lead them to believe they can keep the outside world at bay forever. Instead of embracing opinions, you shut out any that don't mirror yours. I never thought I'd say this, but you're a Type A, ego-maniacal man who would lead his people to extinction rather than listen to a voice that isn't your own."

He smacked his palm with his fist. "Mystic Ridge is four hundred years old. This town has been through and survived change. But do we have to jump at every opportunity that looks like gold? No! This town is too important. Outsiders wouldn't understand."

She stepped back affronted. "That seems to be your claim to fame. I made it out and did something for myself."

His sobering gaze filled her with longing and his anger suddenly subsided. "I'm proud of you," he said.

She stepped forward and grabbed his hands. "I know you are. Please, Peter. Listen to the ideas I have and let me show you how I can help our town."

He turned her hands over and grazed his fingers over her manicured nails. Angel drew them back, knowing he struggled with her L.A. image. "Why do you care? You don't live here. Your parents are going to be traveling. So what's your vested interest?"

Angel brought her hand to her heart. "I care. Mystic Ridge is my home. My roots run deep here."

He gave a disbelieving snort and stepped onto the porch. "You care enough to represent a company who could care less about your roots, except to buy them at the lowest price. Your type of caring is more than we need. Thanks anyway."

He bounded down the steps and started slowly up the winding walkway. The automatic lights attached to the carport flickered on and gave him guidance as he headed toward the grassy knoll.

Angel stood on the porch too. "Where's your truck?"

He shoved his hands deep into his pockets, still walking. "A mile back."

Angel took the stairs one at a time, unable to give up. "What's wrong with it?"

"Dead battery. Go home, Angelina."

"Go home, Angelina," she mimicked. "I'm grown. I can walk beside you if I feel like it."

"No."

"No," she mimicked again.

"Angelina."

"Angelina."

"Hardly the mature woman I expected."

Angel scooped up some dead acorns and pelted him with them. "I'm not scared, you are."

"Angel," he warned.

She threw the last one, then bolted.

Peter caught her within seconds and had her arms pinned to her sides. "You never knew when to stop playing games," he said, his body stiff against hers.

Their breath puffed little white clouds. "This isn't a game to me. Give me a chance. One week to show you the potential of this company. One chance is all I ask."

"A chance to get everyone's hopes up and dash them when this doesn't come through? A chance to divide the town and make us enemies? I can't allow that to happen."

"I promise—"

"To love, honor and cherish—" he supplied.

At her questioning look, he said, "That's what it's going to take. Promise me you won't promise anything you can't deliver and I'll give you one week of my time. You don't have the power to do that, do you, Angel? Mystic Ridge is special. We have our quirks and our faults, but they're unique to us." He let her go, brushed his hands along her arms. "If you only saw Mystic Ridge through my eyes you'd understand."

"Deal."

His wistful expression closed. "Deal what? Oh, no. I'm a busy man and I don't want to hear you preaching to me about your project."

Angel rubbed the cold air that dusted her arms. "Come on. You were always, if nothing else, fair."

He looked doubtful, like a man with the weight of the world on his shoulders. Angel wanted to smooth the worry lines from his forehead and tell him everything would be all right. But she couldn't. She'd compromised herself and him once today. Another time could have far reaching consequences.

"What did today mean?"

"I wanted to call this afternoon a mistake, Peter. It wasn't. But it can't happen again."

She struggled to speak while fighting the urge to give in to her riotous emotions. "I don't want you to think I'm trying to manipulate you with sex." He closed the distance between them. "We share something. A special bond that has surpassed time and distance. But—"

Serious eyes regarded her. "Can't happen again."

"So we have a deal, right?"

"Deal."

Angel touched his arms briefly. "Good. "I'll drive you home before we freeze to death."

"In that little bucket of tin?"

"Does zero to sixty in four point five seconds."

"Really," he said, male appreciation overriding his own objection.

Angel tossed the keys and gave him a wide berth. She didn't look over her shoulder, just hoped he'd follow.

She waited at the car and was pleased when he opened the passenger door for her.

CHAPTER EIGHT

Monday morning arrived bringing blustery winds, freezing pipes, and reserved moods. As it was, the parking lot of his office was full of people who'd heard the grapevine gossip.

Immediately, Peter regretted his hasty decision to accept a ride from Angel this morning. On the surface all was normal, but to most of the men and women watching her park the car, he looked like he was in bed with the enemy.

Before the car had fully stopped, Peter had the door open, his heeled boot digging into the gravel. Angel braked and Peter indicated with a jerk of his thumb. "Park in visitors."

She glanced out as he hefted himself up.

"Peter?"

He had to stoop to see inside the car. "Yep?"

"That says Visitor parking, five minutes. Will I get towed?"

"Let's see, Angel. My father owns the tow truck. I think you're pretty safe."

Seeing her surprise, he backpedaled. "Sorry. That wasn't called for."

He couldn't keep his eyes from straying to her chocolate colored turtle neck, black vest over denim jeans. She'd piled her hair on top of her head in a loose band and had traded her yellow shades for black rimmed glasses that looked useless except to make her more beautiful.

"Lots of people to see you, huh?"

He glanced out the windshield. "Promises to be a full day. I'd better go."

"Meet you inside," she called cheerfully, but he closed the door firmly. Being with Angel made him want to relax and share the inconsequential events of his day.

Focus, he told himself and strode up to several families that greeted him with grave stares. "Mornin'. How long have you folks been waiting?" he said to pregnant Linda Clay Emerson, LulaMae's great grand-daughter.

"Just awhile. Came to talk to you 'bout something."

He clasped her hand and shared his strength as she waddled up the stairs.

Inside, he eased her into Brenda's chair and looked around for his secretary. Nowhere in sight and the rooms were ice cold. He swore silently, stripped off his wool jacket and tucked it around Linda's legs. He could see his breath even inside the building.

The door opened behind them, letting in a full gust of cold wind.

He looked into Linda's friendly eyes. "Don't get this kind of treatment at home, Peter. Kinda nice. Thanks."

"Well don't get too used to it," her husband Sherman said from behind. He came over and kissed Linda on the forehead and shook Peter's hand.

Peter adjusted the thermostat and joined the couple. "What you lookin' at, Sherm? You want the shirt off my back?"

"That piece of rat's nest? How long you had that? Since high school?"

"Probably, good friend." The familiarity eased tension and Peter knew Sherman would hear him out before drawing any conclusions. "Lot of people still outside?" Sherman nodded. "Yep. Might as well let us all in. We all want to know the same thing."

Angel walked in laden with bags followed by the Terry, Hodges, Jackson and Henry families. A few stragglers eased in seeking truth and warmth.

"Everybody, go into the big room over there. I promise the heat will kick on in a minute." Peter took the paper satchels from Angel's arms and put them in the kitchenette. The noise outside the tiny alcove rose as people talked weather and the impending holidays. The undercurrent of worry was about jobs and the future.

"What's all this?"

"Just a few snacks and drinks to make everyone comfortable." Angel bent down and started opening cabinets. "Coffeemaker?"

Focused on her assured movements, he almost missed her question then pointed to the counter. "Kettle. That's the best I've got. I'd better get this impromptu meeting started. Can you handle this?"

"No problem." She opened a box and pulled out a batch of homemade sticky buns. "Delicious," he exclaimed in a hushed tone. Peter popped one into his mouth and savored the flavor of Mystic Ridge's home-made bread and syrup confection. "Bribery isn't going to work."

Angel's serene smile kicked his libido. She wiped his mouth with the tip of her finger.

"I never thought it would. I'll be there in two shakes."

Peter solicited Sherman's help, rounded up chairs and filled the boardroom with as many people as the room could hold. Some of them had traveled many miles, and he didn't want to turn them away without giving them the answers they deserved.

He settled the children in Brenda's office with a box of sticky buns, and plugged in her portable TV so they could watch the purple dinosaur prance around. For some who lived high in the mountains, this was their first glimpse of TV since visiting the local pedi-atrician once a year.

Peter entered the boardroom and looked at the folks that depended upon him. He stood against the wall and gestured for an older gentleman to take his seat.

"Let me just start by saying I know why you've come and I know you want answers."

Angel slipped into the room with steaming cups of coffee and a platter of fresh buns. Eager eyes devoured the food and happy hands made quick selections. When she received a disappointed look from those that didn't receive any, she smiled reassuringly.

"Don't worry, I've got lots more." She turned her seductive smile on Peter. "I didn't mean to interrupt. Please, go ahead."

But from the gracious and thankful looks she received, he knew he wouldn't have their attention until everyone had been served. Peter headed toward the door. "I'll help so we can get on with the discussion."

In her comfortable clothes, Angel didn't stand out against the worn overalls that was pretty much the dress code of Mystic Ridge citizens.

They worked side by side for a few seconds and as she hoisted a tray onto her palm and fingered the other one into her hand, she glanced up and met his gaze. "What?"

"Homemade sticky buns and coffee are not going to sway my decision."

"I know."

Taken aback by her abrupt no-nonsense response, he didn't have a witty comeback. "Just so you know."

"I believe I said I did."

He wanted to say how much he appreciated her help, but thought better of it. Her help would likely destroy Mystic Ridge.

"Let's get this over with. I don't have all day."

"After you," she said and swung the trays shoulder high.

Angel's calm disarmed him and he returned to the room with a full coffeepot.

After dispensing the refreshments, Angel assumed a post in the back of the room. Good. Out of the way.

"Folks, I know you've come because word has spread that Snowden Glass is closing," Peter began.

Several people around Angel offered her a hand pat of sympathy, which annoyed Peter. That wasn't supposed to be a pity party. He was ready to expound upon the argument that Mystic Ridge didn't need the Dyer Corporation. He wanted to share with citizens how they could make it on their own. But with Angel, his nemesis, garnering support, he had to change tactics. Peter regained their attention when he loudly cleared his throat.

"What you've heard is true. Snowden Glass is closing. But we will survive. And not necessarily because we embrace a new corporation. Mystic Ridgeians are strong. This town was built on the backs of freed slaves without commerce from the outside."

"Are you saying we should be thankful we're about to lose our jobs and glad our children will have no other choice but to be farmers? I don't want that for them. Farming is a hard life."

Angry stares and restless movements expressed their discomfort. Heat grew on the inside of his collar. "Not at all," Peter said. "I'm suggesting that we band together before settling for the first company that offers to build here."

"Tell us about the offer. Who is it?" Sherman wanted to know.

"The Dyer Corporation." Angel spoke up then fell silent.

"Give us as much information as you have."

Peter reluctantly nodded his head.

"Dyer builds large variety stores that have everything from clothes to jewelry to food. It's an all-inclusive shopping experience that has been successful in fourteen other cities."

"Woo-oow," said the women in the room.

Peter stared at the back of everyone's head and wondered when he'd lost control.

"Just a minute, Angelina."

Everyone turned to him. "I don't want to get into the details until we have all the facts. Besides, before it can be brought up before a committee, the board members have to discuss whether they believe the company is good for the entire town as well as the ramifications to the state."

Not a single person moved.

Angel filled the silence. "It seems only fair to let everyone know where we are."

Many of them agreed. "Yeah. We're always the last to know."

Angel gave details about her hopes for Dyer and what they'd been able to accomplish with other small cities.

She spoke in a language they understood but even as she gave them information, she was careful not to raise false hopes. Peter found himself listening, wanting to know more.

When Angel finished talking, people were shocked at the financial possibilities. They could be managers, and work regular hours. The earning potential seemed endless and it was hard for Peter not to allow himself to hope what tax revenue would do for the town.

"This is just talk and supposition," he added, deflating the thin layer of hope many had. "Come to the meeting if you can next Wednesday night. We'll know a lot more then."

"Try to see the forest through the trees, Peter," Linda said. "We need a business to save Mystic Ridge. They might not have approached us the right way, but we have you and Angel to protect us. Think about it." She pushed slowly to her feet. "All right, everybody. Let's let them get to work."

When everyone filed out of the office and to their respective cars, Peter noticed the flashing fight on the phone and answered the messages. Brenda had called, explaining she was sick and couldn't make it in. He smirked. She'd be disappointed she'd missed all the fun.

He hurried through the rest of the messages, all from concerned people wondering what the next move was.

Peter wished he knew. He didn't like Dyer's approach and didn't trust them. One thing he'd learned was to follow his instincts. But beyond the money and growth potential, he saw the new schools and hospitals that could be built. He saw paved and not gravel roads. He saw a town teeming with renewal, spirit and life. Rising, he walked back into the conference room.

Angel was cleaning up and didn't say a word as he filled the sink with platters and empty cups.

They worked side-by side, Angel washing, him drying. The scene was almost too domestic. Angel, elbow deep in soapsuds, him coming up behind her for a free feel.

Peter put the breaks on his thoughts, like a race car driver with a warning flag. "Do you agree with Linda?" he finally asked, Ruth's glass platter tight in his hands.

Angel looked at him with the eyes of an angel. "About you not seeing the forest through the trees?"

Impatient, he stared at her. "Why are you making me work so hard? Yes."

"You have foresight and you have great instincts, but in this particular instance, you're operating on an emotional level that can be or will be a hindrance in the future." She dried her hands on a cloth and extricated the platter from his hands. "I'm not the enemy, Peter."

"Never said you were."

Angel packed the plate in a special-made vinyl container. She moved throughout his space with confidence and ease. He leaned against the sink, drawing the dishtowel across another plate and wondered how long it would be before she took it and dried it to her satisfaction. Self-assurance radiated from her, making her sparkle.

For a second his thoughts returned to the meeting and his unusual level of annoyance. Then he realized why. She'd charmed them.

Angel was a real beauty. The kind of woman other women wanted to emulate, from her hair to her style of dress. But that hadn't been what had impressed the people today. Her face had been void of make-up, her hair style simple, her clothes generic. But her voice and her words had held them captive, offering them hope in a time of trouble. Even he couldn't be sure he'd given them that.

"Did you ever consider how many jobs this opportunity could bring to Mystic Ridge?"

"Probably thousands." Even as he wanted to reject the possibilities, Peter had to know what he was in for.

She shrugged. "Maybe not that many initially, but eventually it could. Ever consider what that type of commerce could do for the economy?"

"Generate thousands?"

"Hundreds of thousands."

"Impressive."

She turned to see if he was patronizing her and Peter laid the plate on the table.

"What is it, Peter?"

"Do you ever wonder why I stayed in Mystic Ridge?" Their eyes locked and she moved slowly to the table and sat. He stayed against the sink, grateful for the distance.

"Yes. Every day since I've been home. I've wondered."

"Because there was nobody like me. That gives legs to your ego-maniacal comment, doesn't it?"

She graced him with a self-deprecating smile.

"Look around you. The town is getting old. The members are retiring, moving, dying off one at a time. I've eulogized so many, I sometimes fear I'm boring everyone with the same stories. After college I never intended to stay. I came home to check on my mother and father and when I walked into their house, they were old. It's like for every year it took me to get my degrees, they'd aged ten. At the time Seymour Plunkett was the council president and while I was home, he died."

"How awful."

"You know how Mystic Ridge is. We shut down for the funeral and I agreed to help his wife get his paperwork into a manner she could understand. Next thing you know, I'm sitting in on meetings for my father and one day I look up, and I'm the president."

"Did you ever want to leave?"

He nodded, pursed his lips. "Sure, lots of times. But it became more a passing fancy rather than a goal. After a while, I stopped thinking about it."

"Would you ever?"

He laid his hands on the table and drew back. "Never had a reason good enough to."

"If you found the right girl?" she sounded shy, but her eyes conveyed her desire for an answer.

"Maybe."

"Have you ever…found her?"

"I thought I had—once. But it didn't work out. So I guess the answer is no."

Angel nodded, seemingly satisfied. She reached out and laid her hand on top of his. Warmth worked its way to his fingers and up his arms. A lightness invaded his head and if she were not in his presence, Peter would have shut his eyes and reveled in the spirit of her touch.

As it was now, he couldn't tear his gaze away. She tilted her head, her eyes soft. "I came back with certain expectations of the town and they were all blown to bits. You've done an excellent job. You were chosen, Peter."

As if burned, Angel jerked her hands away and pushed to her feet.

He stood too, wanting to go to her, misunderstanding her resistance to the unusual but heady power that connected them.

"Oh my, I never thought—"

"What, Angel?"

She waved her hand and backed toward the hallway leading to the front of the office. "Nothing. I need to make a couple of private phone calls." She swallowed. "Is there one available?"

Peter felt strange looking at her so closely, but she'd been affected as well. She'd insisted on the rule of noninvolvement, and while he thought it prudent, his body and mind told him different. "You can use my office."

"I just need to get my briefcase from the car and I'll be right back."

Hurrying up the hallway, Angel's boots clicked in decisive steps. Even in her confusion, she sounded self-assured.

Clearing off his desk, Peter gathered his Rolodex and laptop. No matter Angel's job, if he were going to save Mystic Ridge it had to start with calls to the remaining landowners in the south bank. It seemed folks needed a reminder as to why owning that property was so important.

CHAPTER NINE

Frigid air chilled Angel's skin, but not enough to cool her own self-directed disbelief. A few more seconds in Peter's presence and she'd have blurted the bizarre tale of her car talking. The word 'chosen' rattled around in her brain. You are the chosen one.

The words had been spoken as if they were meant for her, and now she'd said them to him. She took a moment to indulge the absurdity of it all. What if they had been meant for her?

What had she been chosen for?

Yes, Peter was the perfect man to lead Mystic Ridge into the twenty-first century. He possessed deep convictions, but balanced his strength with sensitivity. Her words to him made sense.

But why me? I'm regular, she argued with herself.

Angel pulled down the skin under her eyes and stared at herself in the rearview mirror. Letting go of her face, her features returned to normal. But her heart hadn't been normal since she'd pulled into town two weeks ago.

She felt as if she were pushing herself up a steep hill with no supports to latch onto and no net to catch her if she fell. Cold, she blew into her hands and considered starting her car, hitting the highway and not looking back. But what would that accomplish? For the second time in her life she'd be running from feelings that scared her.

Her feelings for Peter were intense. Even after fifteen years. She groaned aloud. What am I doing? Am I doing the right thing for the people of this town? Yes! The answer pressed in on her, leaving no alternative but to believe.

Relieved, she grabbed the door handle, startled as Peter stood there, concern bright in his eyes. "Considering an escape route?" he said, eyeing the Atlas she'd pulled onto her lap.

"Not leaving until my job is done."

"You're leaving town right after that, huh?"

"I've got a job waiting," she said with little conviction. She cleared her throat and looked away.

"That's important."

"Yes, it is." Suddenly Angel wished he'd say the words that hung thick like humidity in the air. She wanted to tell him she didn't have a reason to stay in Mystic Ridge. Her parents had recently bought a RV and were planning vacations—without her.

She wanted to tell him that whatever connected them, was so strong she couldn't sleep at night for wanting to be near him. But Peter stood silently. Emotionless, stoic and strong. As much as a part of her wanted to, she couldn't love him. He'd break her heart. He'd already done it once when he refused to leave Mystic Ridge fifteen years ago.

Peter stuck out his hand and she reached for it. "You'd better get inside. I won't have sympathy even if you end up with a touch of frostbite."

She got out of her car, laptop in hand and Peter draped a thick wool sweater, several sizes too big, over her shoulders.

"Ever heard of a coat?" He shoved his hands in his pockets as they walked back up the stairs.

"Zip it, smarty."

He held the door for her. "That mouth is dangerous. Use my office. It's ready."

At Brenda's desk, Angel put down the laptop and shrugged off the sweater. She held it out to him, missing the heat, yearning for his touch. To touch him would take so little effort, but she made herself stand still. "Thank you. I'm warm now."

"Really?" He grabbed the wool, then discarded it with a flick of his wrist. Peter stood so close, they shared one breath, then two. "Sure you couldn't get any warmer?"

"Probably."

"But you don't want to."

"Peter, we're not on the same side. I don't want you to hate me when this is over."

"Could never hate you." Her gaze flickered to his. Peter's eyes were hooded, his stance casual, the heat emanating from his body anything but. He reached up, fingered a curl, twining it, guiding her forward until they were chest to chest.

"This is dangerous," she whispered. "Don't know if I can keep things separate."

He smoothed back the mass of curls and smiled gently when they popped back at him. "Me either. One day this will be dealt with."

She gazed up at him. "I know."

"Could have serious consequences."

Angel nodded, not trusting her voice.

Peter stepped back. "The office is yours. In about an hour, we'll head out."

Pulling in a hearty breath, she tried to act as if her emotions weren't the object in a crazy ping-pong game. "Where will we start?"

"You'll see. One hour." He ducked out and headed toward the kitchen.

Sitting behind his desk, Angel plugged in the computer and answered e-mail. The partner she worked with at Dyer had left several messages and she called him first. "Bryce, Angel Snowden. By any chance have you sent surveyors out here?"

"Sure have, Angie." Bryce's quick rush of words filled every empty space. "Look, you've been there a week. Have you got the other parcels secured? Tell you what. Are you near a fax machine? Send those documents on over and I can have the boys back out there as early as tomorrow."

"Hold on a second," she said, trying to slow him down. Unease settled around her and she suddenly couldn't tell him about the three parcels she'd already acquired. It seemed wrong to give Bryce that information. "According to my notes, we were just in the acquisition stage. This hasn't even gone through all the channels yet. Much less to the point of hiring surveyors. I mean," she laughed, "this could all fall apart, and then what?"

"This can't fall apart. Angie, have you got the land secured?"

"No," she lied, stunned that he'd gone behind her back. What else had been done since she'd been away from the office? At that very moment she understood Peter's resistance in wanting to do business with Dyer.

A long pause stretched into an uncomfortable silence.

"Bryce, the people are reluctant to sell family land, and understandably so. We need time to work on them."

"What have you been doing?' His voice rang with thinly veiled contempt. "You've had plenty of time."

She drew her hands through her curls and massaged her scalp. A monster headache was on the way as she stalled him. "Don't worry. I'm meeting with some people who I believe will donate their land. I hope to have several parcels before the end of the week."

Angel imagined Bryce in his usual state. Blond hair spiked, sky-blue shades over his blue eyes, feet on his desk.

"Define several, Angie. Mall-mart is ready and waiting for the green light. We'll have bulldozers in there before you can say commission check! Come on, girl. Get-it-to-ge-ther! How many can we count on by the end of this week? Five or six? That's all we need. Those other hillbillies will sell when they see there's no hope."

Images flashed in her mind of Linda and Sherman, Jesse Transom and Peter. LulaMae Clay! The callous way Bryce spoke of them chilled her blood.

"Bryce! Don't you say one more disrespectful thing about these people again. We're partners on this project, but don't think I won't demand that you be removed. Is that understood?"

Angel could only imagine what was going through his little pea brain, but she didn't care.

"Sure, Angie," he replied, conciliatory. "I'm just anxious to get this underway."

"Is that all?" Angel demanded.

"We need the zoning requests. That rinky—sorry, town council president has been sitting on them for months now."

"He has?" she said surprised Peter hadn't mentioned them. Maybe he knew more than he was letting on.

"Don't tell him they're for us or he'll drag his feet into eternity." His tone dipped. "How is it, Angie? Is it just killing you to be in that one-horse town?" Though he tried to sound sympathetic, he failed miserably.

"I'm fine, Bryce."

"A lot hinges on securing this land," he continued. "You know this south bank was grand-fathered to these people by some ancient governor and can't be developed except as a whole. Essentially, if we don't have an entire chunk, it's worthless. Do your job, Angie, and call me at the end of the week."

"My name is An—"

The phone clicked in her ear. She prepared to hang up when her voice mail beeped and indicated another message had been left.

The company's vice-president wanted her to locate a new headquarters for a dessert company in the Maryland area. Did she have any suggestions?

"No," she answered aloud, rubbing her fingers over her forehead as sites came to mind. She dialed his number, praying to leave a message, but he picked up on the second ring.

"John? Angel Snowden."

"Great hearing your voice, stranger. How goes it?"

"Busy and I've only got a minute. I've got a couple of sites for the dessert company. Got a pen?"

"Shoot."

Angel quickly listed the sites and gave an update on the status of the Mall-mart account. She debated asking for Bryce to be reassigned, but decided against it. He was a good partner, who was entitled to make one mistake.

"Anything else," John said after she completed the report.

"No, except if you're interested in buying a glass company, I know where you can get one cheap."

"What kind of glass? Windows?"

"No. Mostly bottles for product." Why had she mentioned this? Luther was closing, not selling. "John, forget I mentioned it. I'd better run."

"Why close the company when you can run it? Ever consider it?"

She shook tier head. "You'd never let me go. Who'd bring you treats?"

"Got a point there," he said slowly. "You sure you're okay?"

Angel smiled. John and his wife Francine had been so good to her. Like second parents since she joined the company five months ago, they'd developed a unique closeness. Nearing retirement age, John wanted her to take his job once he left and Angel aspired to one day rule the roost.

If John were asking her if she were okay, she must sound pretty bad. She mentally kicked her mood up a notch and put some cheer into her voice.

"Everything's fine. I'd better run. Kiss Francine for me."

"You got it, kiddo. Hey, one last thing."

"Yeah?"

"What's the local specialty? Anything to eat?"

Angel smiled. She'd never met a man who loved sweets as much as John. "Let's see. Oh, how about a case of Mystic Ridge's homemade, manufactured and bottled syrup? This stuff is delicious. In fact, the bottles come from my step-father's factory."

"Great! Take care and call soon."

Opening her laptop, Angel lost herself in answering email and didn't look up until a discreet knock sounded at the door.

Peter poked his head in. "You about ready?"

More e-mail waited, but she needed to focus on her job and get more parcels of land. Then this deal would be secure. "Sure am. Get much done?" she asked, as she stood and stretched.

Peter watched her, interest written all over his face. "Some," he said in a guarded tone.

"You received zoning requests regarding the south bank. What did you do with them?" she asked, afraid he'd already made the decision to deny them.

"We have an agreement, Angel. I intend to abide by

She zipped her computer into the leather case and lifted it off the desk. Coming around she prepared to pass, but he took the computer from her hand and stepped back into the doorway.

"Doesn't have to be this way. You could see things my way and make it easy on yourself."

He threw his head back and laughed. "I'm up for anything you can throw my way." Now this was the Peter she remembered. When they were kids, they'd found so much to laugh about.

Since she'd returned, she'd missed his insatiable sense of humor. He was so serious now.

Things must have changed when he took over the town. Perhaps he was living an unfulfilled existence because of the noble spirit that ran through his veins. More than ever she wanted him to be happy.

"What's first on your agenda?" She passed him and he reached around her. For an instant Angel thought he was going to wrap her in his arms. Instead he flipped the light switch, casting the room into semi-darkness.

"First thing is my truck. My father's got it at the garage and said he would have the battery in this morning."

Angel checked her watch and nodded. "No problem. And after that?"

"We hang out."

"Ooo-kay." She followed him through the office and watched as he juggled her laptop and the vinyl covered bag of platters.

"Let me help you." Angel took the vinyl bag of plates and was grateful they hadn't touched. They seemed to possess a connection because every time he touched her, she felt that warm-in-the-tub-feeling.

Angel gasped and brought her hand to her throat. Just like in the car. It felt right.

"You okay?" he said from behind her. "Angel?"

"Fine." She patted her warm cheeks. "I know this is going to sound funny, but something weird happened to…a friend awhile back and it just came to mind."

He guided her outside and when she strutted to the driver's door, he looked offended.

Snow would fall in Mystic Ridge before she asked him to drive her car again, and everyone knew it hadn't snowed in the small town in over five years. Angel flipped her hand in an offhand manner. "One day she was alone in her car and she said it talked."

"What did it say?" he said without a hint of a smile.

She debated telling him for fear she'd reveal herself as the "friend." But he seemed to be listening with only half an ear. His gaze roamed the streets as she pulled out of the lot.

"Wait a sec," he said, hopped out to move some garbage cans onto the curb, then got back in. "All right. So go ahead with your story."

"She said it said something about her being chosen." He stared right into her soul. So much for him not being interested. "To do what?"

"She doesn't know."

"Maybe to lead. Maybe to deliver a message. Everyone has a purpose here on earth and sometimes it's just enough to know God put you here to serve." He spoke with such reassurance, suddenly the experience didn't seem so weird.

Angel drove through the town that had been built like rings on a tree. All the businesses started in the center and rotated out until they met farmland and miles of nothing but trees.

Beautiful even in the winter, the bare tree branches had been strung with white Christmas lights, and happy black elves painted on the doors of the local businesses.

They cruised twinkling Main Street and waved to people as they passed. Peter assisted her failing memory with reminders of each person's family, and updated her on the latest happenings in their lives.

When Peter directed her to the Apothecary to pick up a prescription for his father, Angel felt like Junior Miss Mystic Ridge, the way everyone carried on about her coming home, and her success in California. Obviously her mother and Luther bragged regularly.

The special feelings didn't dissipate when Peter whisked her back into the car when some teenage boys tried to pick her up.

"They want the car, not me," she said, flattered by their attention and even more by Peter's jealousy.

"Making it with a beautiful woman who owns a car is a dream come true for these boys. Don't smile. You're encouraging them."

She waved and winked, causing them to follow along the planked sidewalk until Angel drove through the intersection. "They're kind of cute."

"Cradle robbing?"

She smirked at his jealous streak. "Hardly," she said breezily. "You're a day past dirt so I wouldn't hate on anyone." He chuckled with her.

Richland Automotives was on the next block and Angel turned right and pulled in behind the senior Richland's truck.

Clothed in a one-piece workman's uniform, Mr. Richland pumped gas into the truck *in* front of her, collected his money and waved them ahead. Angel put down her window and got a full blast of cold air in the face.

"How are you two doing today? Gettin' along?" Angel laughed. "Of course."

Peter snorted at his father's comment and gestured toward the garage. "Where's Sherman? I thought he was on today."

"You know Linda's going to drop that baby any day. Every time I turn around she's calling, thinking it's time. Women," he said, slightly exasperated.

"My truck ready?"

Mr. Richland took a rag from his pocket and rubbed bugs from the windshield. "Naw, your truck ain't ready. I told you to bring it in for a tune-up last month and you didn't, so I got it in the garage gettin' fixed right."

"Dad, I need my truck."

"Why? Seems to me you got a pretty good situation right here."

"I can't rely on Angel to drive me around town. Give me your keys. I'll take your truck until mine is fixed."

"Think again. You can't borrow my truck."

Angel couldn't suppress her smile any longer. Nothing had changed. Peter and his father had always bickered but the love between the two ran deeper than the sea. Especially since Mrs. Richland had died so early in Peter's life.

"Why can't I borrow your truck? If I recall, I bought you that truck."

Mr. Richland slapped his thigh with the rag and stuffed in back into his pocket. "You bought it, but you don't own it."

"Dad—"

"Angel, you don't mind riding Peter around until I can fix his truck, do you?"

"When will it be done?"

"Wednesday."

"Wednesday!" they exclaimed at the same time. "Afternoon," he said, flexing his thick fingers.

"That's over a week. What are you doing to it? Rebuilding the thing from the inside out?"

Mr. Richland waved to the occupant of the blue Pontiac Grand Am that had pulled in behind them. "You ain't a paying customer, son. I got to take care of people who got money," he said and went to greet his customer. He walked around the rear bumper and turned up at Peter's window.

"What now? You want to reupholster the seats while you're at it?"

"Give me my prescriptions before I decide to put monster wheels on it." He received the bag and with surprising quickness, pinched Peter's cheek, then went back to his customer.

Angel howled at Peter's embarrassed expression. He soon joined her but kept shaking his head.

"Where to?" she asked.

"Rural route 7 is where we'll begin. That man drives me crazy," he said with such a touch of affection she reached out and patted his hand.

"He means well. Just think. you'll have a brand new truck next week."

"You don't have to chauffeur me around. I can borrow Sherman's old Tempo. I don't want to put you out."

She shook her head, drawing back her hand. It tingled as threads of awareness shot to the center of her body. Her breath caught as she tried to out-wait the thrumming between her thighs.

"It's not a problem. We vowed to see Mystic Ridge your way, so it doesn't really matter who drives. Right?"

He rolled up his window and sat back. "I guess not, but it just doesn't feel right."

"What?"

"You driving me around."

Angel stared out the windshield, the car dipping into the holes in the gravel road that represented the rural route. It was about to snow. "Do you want to drive?"

He shrugged, sounding casual. "It only seems right."

"Fine." Angel pulled over and pushed back the seat. He seemed happy behind the wheel even if his knees were drawn up to the dash.

"Go easy. My car has never seen roads like this before. We're completely at your mercy."

"Never tell a man you're at his mercy," his voice rubbed her like strong but gentle hands. Excitement burned her belly and anticipation made her look at him from the corner of her eye.

"Why?"

"It's an invitation too hard to resist. Believe me."

The thrumming increased. Angel drew her knees together and squeezed.

Time was closing in, Dahia knew, and Angel needed a boost. She heard Angel's thoughts and felt her attraction to Peter, but at this pace they wouldn't get married before 2002. She glanced over her shoulder at Nefertiti and Sheba who were in quiet conference with God and focused her attention on Angel.

For them, she said to herself, I will help Angel.

She began her council with Angel's heart. "Open your eyes. God gave them to you to see. Close your mouth, for if you are speaking you cannot hear. Listen with your heart. It hears what your ears cannot. Succeed! You are the best of us all."

Rain drops dappled the glass on the front of the rolling contraption and Angel and Peter drove on.

CHAPTER TEN

Lead seemed to fill Angel's shoes and her legs felt as if they were made of rubber. Her face burned from being in the harsh winter sun and her jaws hurt from smiling.

Angel climbed out of bed on the ninth day of seeing Mystic Peter's way and wanted to collapse. For over a week, he'd taken her to the most remote corners of Mystic, parts she'd never known existed.

They'd met farmers, cattlemen, cowboys and modem day shepherds. In some places there was no running water and in others, the locations were so remote, the people didn't come to town in the winter.

Peter knew them by name, their children and even their animals. He knew of their struggles and never showed up empty-handed.

In a twenty-pound back pack, Angel carried food and bottles of medicine, while Peter carried the other two. No matter where they turned up, everyone was grateful to see him, and never sent him home without something for him or his father or Brenda.

During the course of the visit, the subject of the south bank would come up and everyone had different opinions. Many didn't want anyone to come in and take over their town. Most lived by the land and didn't want it destroyed. But there were some who welcomed change and wished them the best.

Angel sat quietly most of the time watching and absorbing. She wanted to explain Dyer's position, but after hearing the initial reactions, found it more prudent to listen.

She saw things, felt emotions she'd never had before and allowed herself to simply absorb.

When Peter introduced her, everyone spoke highly of her step-father and mother, and their sincerity was something new to Angel. She'd been away so long, she didn't identify with Snowden Glass. That was her step-father's enterprise. But seeing the impact on the town made her realize how much of a loss it would be and reconfirmed her belief that her ideas could help.

Stepping gingerly into the shower, she groaned when the massage sprayer soothed her aching muscles. Tomorrow night was the town meeting and it promised to be a doozy. She needed all of her strength.

Pulling on loose cotton pants and a warm sweater, Angel sank onto the kitchen chair and looked at her bare piece of toast. She dribbled out a bit of syrup, started to eat and turned her attention to her e-mail.

Fourteen were labeled 'analysis' and she downloaded each one, then printed.

Noticing the empty plate, she popped more bread into the toaster, then added syrup. She nibbled at the toast and sat down, licking her finger for a wayward drip. Somebody ought to market this stuff. It was delicious.

Her stomach grumbled for more, but Angel took the syrup and bread and shoved it all in the refrigerator. Out of sight, out of mind.

Gathering the reports, she glanced through, liking what she saw.

A knock at the door brought her attention up and she could see Peter's large frame through the clear paned glass.

Her heartbeat quickened and she took a swallow of lukewarm tea. For the past nine days, she'd been in firm control of her libido, but she had to work hard to keep her guard up. Today would require extra strength. Being together so much, they'd grown closer than she thought possible.

Tossing the briefcase and reports onto the dining room table she hurried to the door and opened it.

"Hey you," he said, stepping in to the kitchen. "You look warm," and after giving her a second glance, "and happy."

Angel couldn't keep a smile from her lips. "I am. Care for some breakfast?"

He shrugged out of his wool jacket. "Sure. What you got cooking?"

They both turned to the spotless daisy covered kitchen and chuckled. "Nothing. But I can fix you something. Won't take but a minute."

"Where's your mother and Luther?"

"She convinced him to take her to D.C. for some shopping. You'll see them tomorrow at the meeting."

She cleared the table of her computer and printer.

"You wouldn't believe I'd been gone fifteen years," she said, coming back into the kitchen. "My room looks like I never left."

Seeing Peter in her mother's kitchen reminded Angel of long ago days when he used to come over and they'd study together.

Suddenly she felt nervous, as if something was about to happen. He watched her with curious eyes. "What are you looking at?" she said.

"Can't look at something pretty?" he said smoothly. "Mmm, compliments. You must be hungry. What do you want to eat?"

"What do you have?"

Angel's muscles screamed in protest as she pulled Canadian bacon, eggs, cheese and a bag of oranges from the crisper. "I've got enough for a good old fashioned breakfast." She unloaded everything on the table. "Or an omelet with freshly squeezed orange juice. I figured we'd eat then go and do whatever you do on a Tuesday."

"I don't want an omelet."

Her head snapped up. "Okay. You want just eggs and grits? I know mother has something in here you like. Don't tell me your taste has changed that—" She stopped mid-sentence and turned to him. A flush of desire hit her suddenly. "What do you want?" she asked, her breath growing shallow in the heat of his gaze.

"You know what I want." His legs were braced open, his arm leaning casually on the table.

Angel looked over the sink and into the backyard. Cold wind whipped around leaves and twigs, but inside the house the temperature had shot through the roof. She took a step toward him. "You want me?"

"Yes."

Joy leapt in her chest and she fought a smile. "Now?"

"Now."

"What happens after that, Peter? How do we move on? We live a country apart—"

"And tonight," he said.

Her objections fizzled. "And?" she swiped at a stray curl.

"Tomorrow."

She moved a step closer. "You work tomorrow."

"I'm sick tomorrow."

"Oh."

"Take off that sweater."

She laughed, suddenly nervous. "Here? In the kitchen?"

"I want to see you." The simple request was filled with such yearning, her heart swelled.

Crossing her hands, she pulled the hem over her head and tugged until free of the garment. It stirred the air on its way to the floor. Her stomach was no longer pancake-flat, but she tingled at his appreciative gaze.

Angel hooked her fingers into her waistband and gave him a questioning look. His gaze moved from her hands to her eyes. She licked her lips and said, "Do you have protection?"

Peter smiled and with agonizing slowness, stretched out long legs, reached into his right pants pocket and withdrew a handful of condoms.

Angel unzipped.

He reached into his left pocket and withdrew another handful of condoms.

She let the pants slip down her legs and stepped from them.

When he reached for his back pocket, she knew she was in for a long day and night.

She walked toward Peter and lifted his face in her hands. She wanted to say what lay on her heart, but her emotions were in a jumble. Instead she kissed him, tasting him as if for the first time. His lips were firm, but gentle, moist and thick, moving with her mouth in a steady beat of loving. His tongue sought hers first, tentatively seeking it for a pleasurable tango.

His broad hands cupped her mid-thigh and leisurely slid up. When his fingers squeezed her butt, Angel broke the kiss to share a breath with him. Her eyelids lifted enough to see desire bright in his eyes. "Peter?" she said, as his fingers hooked the band of her Victoria's Secret panties and pulled them part of the way down.

"Yes?" He cupped her ass and squeezed.

The onset of a climax started to roll through her body. "I want you now."

He picked her up and Angel had just enough time to grab a handful of condoms before his mouth locked on hers and they stumbled into her room and onto her bed.

In a deft move, he tugged her panties off as Angel pushed at his sweater and jeans. Skin to smooth skin, a thin barrier separating their most intimate parts, Peter pulled her astride him and impaled her, sending her over again.

The thrill of climaxing didn't completely ebb as they established an aggressive pump and thrusting motion that had the bed knocking against the wall. Angel didn't care if they shook the house down. She only wanted to be with Peter and give him all that was inside of her.

Their mouths met, wide and hot, moving to satisfy the insatiable. He held her with his arms wrapped in hers, his hands gripping her backside, his manhood to the hilt when a growl tore from his chest.

With all his might Peter pulled her to him, his teeth grazed her collarbone, and he burst inside of her.

CHAPTER ELEVEN

Peter held onto to Angel as if his life depended upon it. He didn't care that he vowed to leave her alone and to handle their situation as he would with any professional. All those plans were shot to hell. How could he keep her with him?

This business had to work. But he didn't want to think of that now with her in his lap, naked, warm, wanting him. He'd never felt better in his life.

Angel felt good. She was so soft, but he wondered about her heart. She had things waiting for her back in California, but he wanted her here in Mystic Ridge. Would that be enough?

Her head rested against his shoulder, her arms around his back. "I think you just tried to kill me."

He laughed, holding her closer. "Well, thank you, Ms. Snowden, I've never been paid such a high compliment."

She moved and her perspiration slick breasts drew a path up his chest. Peter groaned and looked into sexy eyes.

"Your eyes say so much more than your mouth ever did. I don't know if I can—"

"Don't say it. Not now, Angel. We're both adults. We can both have our own agendas and still find a way to make this work."

She pressed her mouth to his, her lips full of affection and tenderness. This was not a kiss good-bye, but one of beginnings. He accepted it, the passion behind it sweeping him into a feeling of well-being.

Her thumbs grazed his cheeks as her forehead rested on his. "I've wanted this for a long time, but I don't want to mess it up."

His body stirred and he laid her down gently. "You can't. We're in this until we decide otherwise?"

"Is that it, Peter? 'Otherwise' decides our future?"

"We do, Angel. You know that." He touched her chest, drawing his finger slowly down the center of her body.

Angel tried to keep her wits about her, but his fingers were driving her closer to ecstasy and further from a level head. She gladly made the leap into pure joy.

After the sun had sunk for the night, Angel and Peter left the room and had their long forgotten breakfast. He watched her constantly, never having seen anyone so sexy.

Clad in a T-shirt and boxer pajama bottoms, she cooked and cleaned the kitchen while he read Dyer's prospectus. She held her breath as he slowly turned the pages of data she'd memorized months ago.

When he finally looked up she gazed at him expectantly.

"So?"

"Impressive."

A sigh of relief flew from her lips and she clapped her hands. "I knew you'd think so. I was thinking we could visit towns where there are Mall-mart stores and perhaps see how they operate on a day-to-day basis. That would raise your level of assurance and show you how this whole concept can work. I don't want there to be a shadow of a doubt. Anywhere."

"I never doubted you."

Angel sat at the corner of the table. "Never once?" He shook his head. "I tried to test you at every phase and you never complained. Not once."

Angel folded the dish towel she'd been holding and placed it on the table. "You tested me? How?"

"I took you every place I thought a city girl might hate. I took you places some aren't proud of. The farms, the mountains, the valleys. You saw what I see. The poor Mystic Ridge. The part I want to help, but can't because that's their life."

"Oh, Peter," she sighed, understanding.

"I know you wonder why I stay. I belong here. I love it here. The good and the bad. The poor and the wealthy. The one stop light and the stop sign nobody wants."

She giggled. "Yeah, that did cause a flap. I like it here, too. I never saw this side of Mystic Ridge before. I guess I was so busy wanting to get out and see the world, I didn't see what was around me."

"And?"

She covered his hand. "I see it now and I want to help. Dyer will hire at least five hundred employees and offer jobs from builders to clerks to managers. This is an awesome opportunity."

Peter took her hand and caressed it. "I wasn't convinced before, but I am now."

Angel flew into his arms. "Thank you," she whispered. "You won't regret this."

"It's not for me," he said gruffly. "It's for Mystic Ridge. But I'm no longer the one you have to convince. There's a town of people and half of them don't want this type of change. I don't like the way the company went about getting the land and I plan to make sure nothing like that happens again. But that doesn't mean they don't have my approval."

"Thank you. Thank you." She kissed his lips, wishing they could share this type of bliss forever. The idea didn't even scare her anymore. Angel smiled against his mouth. "Come back to bed with me."

"My pleasure."

She took his hand, led him to her room and closed the door.

Nefertiti, Dahia and Sheba watched over the couple with joyous smiles on their faces.

Dahia moved first, extending her palm. The lifeline was eel black and deep. Nefertiti extended hers and smiled her satisfaction. Nervous, Sheba extended her hand and wanted to collapse in tears. Her lifeline was still sandy brown.

To her surprise, Dahia came and gave her a sad pounding on the shoulder.

Somehow Angel wasn't where she needed to be and time was running out. "Where have we failed her?" Sheba demanded, afraid she had not only chosen wrong, but not fully blessed Angel with the skills needed to instill knowledge and truth. "This is my fault."

"This is not your fault. Angel must be in love, and possess all the skills to instill the legacy. We have time, but I admit she needs a nudge," Nefertiti said. "What about her mother? Ruth was intelligent and perhaps she would have succeeded had her husband not been killed in that war."

"That is true. He was quite a fighter. Those types always did attract me."

Sheba and Nefertiti looked at Dahia shocked. "What? I cannot like a man?"

"I thought you only liked them for gouging lamb from your teeth with the tips of their heads," Nefertiti said. "Unless there is a good battle going on."

"Oh, they are worth so much more than that," Dahia said, unexpectedly.

They both looked at her and giggled, but then their laughter drifted off as they looked at Angel.

"She is about to experience a fall she might never recover from. How can we prepare her for this challenge? Prove that this test and love can co-exist?" Dahia said, sounding weary.

Nefertiti reached out for their hands and they locked.

"Our strength, our power, our love will be her guiding force. She will feel us in her soul and she will do the right thing. She is the chosen one."

Lightning flashed across the heavens and the queens prayed, infusing love into the thunderbolts and sent them rocketing to Angel's heart.

CHAPTER TWELVE

Peter left Angel in the late morning hours on Wednesday. He'd stayed with her nestled in their den of happiness and she was glad they'd been together. It wasn't just that he was a fantastic lover. Peter made her feel a wholeness she hadn't ever felt before.

Her parents had decided to visit some relatives in the Virginia area and wouldn't be back until right before the meeting. Angel had taken advantage of their absence and thoroughly enjoyed Peter's company. She let him out the door with a toe-curling kiss, and decided to spend the day working on her pitch for Mall-mart.

The town council would have plenty of data to make a sound decision. She loved Mystic Ridge and wanted her place of birth to be a place of pride and joy for generations to come.

Stopping in her tracks, Angel felt the first swell of love and let the odd feeling overtake her.

What am I saying? She sank onto a kitchen chair. Sure I love this town, but do I want to stay?

The thoughts didn't shock or repulse her. In fact, she felt lighter and happier than she had in a long time.

She looked around the kitchen and decided to clean up first, answer e-mail then write up her report. Given that the sun went down early, the meeting was scheduled for six o'clock. That would allow enough time to go to town and use the copy machine if necessary and then enjoy the afternoon.

Getting down to business, Angel had the house sparkling in two hours.

Showered and dressed, she gathered boxes of paperwork and set them out making sixteen sets of individual packets of information. In each she included photographs of other locations and color photos of what the property would look like.

Proud of the projection information regarding jobs, she placed a sheet on each packet and filled in the folders with other pertinent information. In an hour she was done and stuffed them into manila folders and back into the box, which she dragged to the porch. Peter still had her car and they had grown accustomed to traveling together. He was supposed to pick her up at five-thirty.

The sky threatened a snowstorm but she prayed it would hold off until Christmas night, only a month away.

This past week she'd driven through the festive town marked with holly and silver garlands. The air was frigid on days, but it helped bolster the holiday spirit.

Though everyone was worried about Snowden Glass closing down, they didn't stop being cheerful and willing to express their glee with the holiday.

Mystic Ridge was so different from California. The seasons changed here and even though spring was months away, a sense of renewal was in the air. Over the past weeks, the citizens had shown her more love and acceptance than she had ever felt in L.A.

Maybe I am just a country girl, she thought as she wiped the counters in her mother and stepfather's kitchen and walked into the deep pantry and looked for a snack. Her-eyes came to rest on a bottle of syrup and she fingered the special design with a wave of sadness. With Snowden Glass closing, this would end too.

Angel closed the door and with it the sad feelings.

Something better was around the corner and she headed into the dining room to get the remainder of her paperwork.

❦

Angel reread each analysis for a second time and couldn't believe her eyes. If Peter ever saw these reports, he'd never agree to allow Mall-mart anywhere near Mystic Ridge.

Detailed information of environmental hazards, waste disposal, unfair hiring practices, increased crime and drug use, and stress on town's resources highlighted each report.

What had she done?

In fifteen minutes, Peter was supposed to pick her up and what was she going to say? I've made a terrible mistake and I'm sorry?

The ringing phone cut into her thoughts. "Angie, baby. It's Bryce. So, what do you have good to tell me?"

"Did you read the reports from the markets we've already moved Mall-mart into?"

"I read them." He sounded confused. "How did you get those? I put them on your desk and was planning to mail them uh, next week."

"John sent them to me. You weren't ever going to let me see these! Bryce, I can't believe you. This isn't going to work. We can't mislead these people into believing this is for their own good. This will destroy Mystic Ridge."

"What will it do to your career, Angie? You ever thought of that? I swear, you sentimental types make my butt hurt. Save the whales. Don't run over the manatee. Grow up, Angie. This is the real world. Join it or stay stuck in your one horse town. I don't care, but you're not going to ruin this sweet-ass commission for me. This is my career, too." He made gurgling noises, then hung up.

The warning sound indicating the phone was off the hook signaled the end of Angel's dream. Sadness and shame worked through her bones making her feel a weariness she'd never felt before. She blamed herself for not knowing the results and for raising the hopes of people she now must let down. It didn't matter that she'd inherited this project when she came on board with the company. She'd brought them to Mystic Ridge and if the town suffered it would be her fault. There was only one thing to do.

Picking up the phone, she dialed and before she could change her mind, she resigned.

When Angel heard a car pull up outside, she grabbed the reports and hurried out the door.

Weighed down with the box, she grabbed the handle of her car door and hopped in. "I've got to tell you something—whoa. You're not Peter."

"Sherman," he said by way of introduction. "We've met. Peter had to get over to the gymnasium and set up some chairs, so I'm filling in."

"Doesn't he have a cell phone? I really need to get in contact with him." Sherman looked at her with patient eyes. "It's vital that I speak with him right away."

He held up his hands seemingly used to hysterical women.

"He has a cell phone, but, no, you can't call him."

"Why not?"

"His cell phone is right here."

Angel muttered an unladylike oath under her breath and she sat back. "I just need to see him before we get started. Can we hurry?"

"He told me to make sure you were taken care of. If you want to get there early, I'm your man. Fasten your seat belt," he said. "I always wanted to drive one of these things fast."

Angel appreciated the glow in his eyes. "Let's see how fast you can make it go."

Thick gray clouds poured great sheets of water from the sky, but that didn't deter nearly every citizen of Mystic Ridge from filling the high school's gymnasium.

This coming together was an event.

The atmosphere was jovial, but most were interested in what was going to happen, rather than say that a change was about to occur.

Angel looked for Peter in the crowd, but couldn't find him. She wanted to scream his name and have him appear at her side, but couldn't without alarming everyone present. So she rushed through the crowd staring into faces until the town council, minus Peter, took their places behind long tables.

Angel took a seat. She had no choice but to tell the truth when the time came.

The cheerleaders had just performed and the band finished up a selection when Peter approached the microphone.

He looked so handsome standing there in black jeans, a brown sweater and a sparkle in his eye. She wanted to rush up to him and tell him he was right and she wrong. But the crowd was immense and she just couldn't add another humiliation to her growing list.

Peter took care of all the other town business and then got to her. Sherman wheeled in a projector and everyone clapped enthusiastically when Peter called her name.

Angel got to her feet, the pit of her stomach down around her ankles. She went through with her presentation and received hearty applause. "But I'm not done," she said and took a sip of water. "There's another side."

She looked into Peter's eyes and felt sadness for what she'd lost and for how she'd made him feel. But the truth was the truth and they deserved to hear it from her.

"Crime in ten of the fourteen cities has increased thirty-four percent. Cities suffer traffic jams when they never used to, and four of the cities report a seventeen percent increase in drug use.

"With the seventy-five families they reportedly bring in, only one in four of those have ever lived in a small town. They stay approximately two years and then move on. This has raised taxes for local home-owners nearly forty-four percent." She pointed to the graph. "This level here, is where Mall-mart pulls their managers." She shook her head. "Not from the locals."

"What about marketing?" Roy Cochran's daughter-in-law asked.

"They have a corporate office in Georgia and based on their past record, they don't generally hire anyone from the outside. Our citizens will be relied upon to provide clerical staff, builders and other—as they put it 'nonessential' staff."

A disappointed murmur filtered throughout the crowd. "There's more." By the time she finished talking, she could have heard a pin drop.

Angel didn't know what she expected, but it wasn't absolute and utter silence. Everyone stared at her wide-eyed yet accepting the truth. She stood at the micro-phone surrounded on every side by people she'd been reunited with and loved, and felt wholly responsible for them being there.

She raised the report in her other hand. "This will not save us. We can only save ourselves. Mystic Ridge has so much to offer herself and I don't believe I took the time to look at its beauty and simplicity before trying to change it. The south bank can only be developed as a whole. Dyer doesn't own enough of the land to do anything with it." The murmur turned to relieved sighs. "This can end here and now. I'm sorry," she said finally.

"You did what you thought best," Maureen Clay said from behind the long table where the council members sat. "You got us rejuvenated and looking at our future. And in the end, you came forward and told us the truth. That's all we can ask for."

Angel thanked them for their support and took her seat, waiting until she could pack her car and leave.

As much as she wanted to stay in Mystic Ridge, she didn't know what she had to offer now. She couldn't not work. That wasn't an option, besides she had bills to pay. And what was there to do in Mystic Ridge? Adding herself to the unemployment statistics just didn't seem fair.

Tears burned behind her eyes, but she would not let them fall even as the crowd applauded her effort and many came to shake her hand. This didn't work out, but something else would, she told herself.

Keeping her gaze off Peter, she sat through his short speech to rally the citizens, and his good wishes for a happy holiday. He promised them he'd find a solution by the first of the year and when Angel looked up, hope shined in his eyes.

They ended with Reverend Benson giving the benediction and the meeting was adjourned.

The gymnasium emptied and the men and kids stacked chairs, while the women packed food and exchanged small gifts. Toddlers lay sleeping in the corner on quilted blankets. A few kept up a crying harmony, and those able to walk were watched by the elders who sat in a circle of canes and stocking feet.

Angel loved it. This was home. No matter what, Mystic Ridge would always be home.

Peter worked with the men stacking chairs and with his gentle manner, offered advice to several of the teens. He looked so handsome in the midst of his followers, he was the chosen one for a reason.

She had to see him, talk to him to apologize for what she'd put him through, but Angel didn't know if she could without crying.

"If you love him, tell him so," her mother said gently.

Angel was startled and surprised to see her mother and Luther. "Mom, Dad. I'm so glad to see you."

Her mother's eyes filled and Luther embraced her and gave her a wet kiss on the cheek. "I love you," she whispered in his ear.

"I've always known," he said emotional. "We want you to stay, Angel."

She shook her head and her father took her face in his hands. "Don't just stay for us. Stay *because* you want to."

"I have to face him and apologize for what I've done. I believed the Dyer Corporation could help Mystic Ridge. Even when Peter objected, I pushed. Once I say what I need to, I have to go."

"You don't have to go," her mother said gently as Peter and the teens pushed dust mops across the gym floor. "You were chosen for Mystic Ridge. We still need you, Angel. You're our bright star. Admission of a mistake shows honor, strength and intelligence. I've never seen you back down. Don't start now. We're going home. I want to see you tomorrow."

"Mother—"

"Goodnight, child of mine."

They passed Peter who seemed intent only on her. He took her hand and led her from the building and helped her into her car. The car hummed and the wipers beat a steady rhythm as they cleared white snowflakes from the windshield.

Angel felt Peter's intensity and didn't know how to respond to it. She wanted to say the words in her heart, but her mouth couldn't speak them.

Everything in her body said 'tell him you love him,' but she couldn't. Couldn't risk his rejection.

She closed her eyes wondering where they were going, but not anxious to end their last evening together. When the car stopped, they were at the top of a hill, a wood cabin before them.

"Where are we?"

"My house."

"Peter, I'm sorry. I—" her voice broke. "I just want to go home."

"Come inside for a minute, please. We need to say some things."

She looked at him, but didn't want to fight. She got out of the car and followed him inside. He flipped a switch and flooded the downstairs with light. In the weeks since she'd been home, Angel had never been to his home.

The log cabin was absolutely beautiful. A large stone fireplace dominated the living room with a staircase against the wall. It led up to a large king-size bedroom that could have been made especially for him.

A bathroom sat off the room as well as a closet and hot tub. She looked up. "You have a very nice home."

"Thank you. Let me show you the downstairs."

Two additional bedrooms were off the kitchen and dining room, and large glass doors looked over the mountainside.

Rain and snow pattered against the roof and water ran down the outside windows insulating them from any disturbance.

Angel walked back toward the dining room where Peter stood in the center of the floor. "Why did you bring me here?"

"I wanted you to see my home. I want you to know that you'd be happy here. With me."

She attempted to talk and her voice cracked. "I can't stay. I failed you and Mystic Ridge."

"You are the most admired woman this town has ever had. Not only did you single-handedly try to effect change, but you saved us from situations that would have hurt us."

He took her hand and led her to the sofa. She looked at her hand locked in his and wanted this moment to last forever.

"We have simple needs, Angel. Mall-mart is too lofty for us, but keeping Snowden Glass open, isn't."

"My father said that," she whispered.

"It seems a man named John thinks so too. At least according to his phone call a while ago."

She smiled through her tears. "My ex-boss."

"From the way it sounds, he has some ideas."

She grasped his hand in hers. "John would."

"In Mystic Ridge," Peter said, "we don't remember old fights and we don't hold grudges. Life is as it is, but you're a part of this town. And me."

"Peter, I nearly destroyed part of our legacy. I acquired land for the Dyer Corporation and was prepared to turn it over to them. How can you forgive me?"

"You didn't, did you?"

"No. I couldn't."

"Then there's nothing to forgive. I love you. You have a much bigger legacy to instill and you started tonight when you admitted you'd made a mistake."

Tears of joy trickled down her cheeks. "I'll get the land back. I promise. Oh, goodness. I quit my job today. What—" She smiled through her tears. "What are you smiling at?"

"You are a courageous, strong woman full of integrity and wisdom and immense strength. I love you very much. Stay," he said.

Angel felt her heart sing and moved to kiss him and she felt all the barriers slip away.

"Marry me, Peter and give me sons that will grow up and love life and their families and their town like you love me."

He drew her into his arms, knowing what they had would last forever. "That's a promise I'd love to keep."

&

Nefertiti, Dahia and Sheba celebrated their joy by dancing late into the day. Decked in ethereal finery, each wore the highest crown bestowed by their Heavenly Father.

Dahia was dressed as any warrior priestess would be. Metal from her neck to her feet, complete with a shiny sword at her side. Sheba lounged on her cloud in shimmering silk, and Nefertiti looked regal in brilliant gold.

"Our work is done," Dahia said as Peter and Angel jumped the broom New Years Eve with barely a minute to spare.

"We almost didn't make it, but Angel is all of us and I could never get anywhere on time. Ask Solomon," Sheba supplied.

"What will you do now, Sheba?" Dahia asked.

"Help lost souls who don't make it all the way here after death."

"That is a good choice for you. I will join the fighting Angel corps. They need leadership!"

Nefertiti and Sheba laughed.

Sheba turned to Nefertiti. "What will you do?"

"I'm glad you mentioned it," she said as she glided toward them. "God used us to instill this legacy and He is very proud. It seems there are Ongs in the tenth dimension who can use our assistance saving their children from peril. God and I thought—"

Dahia and Sheba rose. "You mean work together again? Are you wicked in the head? She wears metal on her chest," Sheba said, moving away from Dahia.

"At least I don't shiver every time a strong Heavenly wind blows. My metal protects me. I cannot do this with this queen who is no more help than a helpless rabbit. I won't," Dahia said.

"I won't," Sheba repeated.

"You will," Nefertiti said, and grabbed their hands.

HOME FOR
THE
HOLIDAYS

BY LESLIE ESDAILE

Humph, that Angel Snowden nearly turned Mystic on its ear...but she had a lot of help from above. Then again, there's nothing strange about that, at least not in Mystic. There's just something about the place that draws people in and changes their lives forever. Just look at that young couple, Collette and Franklin. Even though their visit started out as an unhappy occasion, by the time the spirits worked their magic neither of them were the same. And a good thing, too. What a ruckus went on up in old Nana Johnson's house. Folks in Mystic are still laughing about it and shaking their heads. And I'd bet money Nana Johnson had a hand in it. Yessir...

CHAPTER ONE

Philadelphia, Pennsylvania...2000

Colette Johnson-Morris sighed as she watched her husband drift off into the routine slumber that always seemed to follow their lackluster lovemaking these days. With twenty minutes to spare before the alarm clock sounded, she reached over to the nightstand and turned off the offending technology, and tried to stave off her physical frustration that was now merging with resilient anger.

She resented the way his long, thick-built chocolate frame seemed to rest, satiated, without a care in the world, and it annoyed her that his easy smile and deep brown eyes could always coax her into this position—agreeing to be unfulfilled. She wondered if he'd rest so peacefully if he had to lie in the wet-spot and hover on the verge of an orgasm that never ignited? It was so easy for men.

But how could one year of marriage have changed so much between them? she worried, as she shuffled to the bathroom. It wasn't always like this. Maybe this was just a six-month-long phase? There was a time when his voice over the telephone would make her mound swell and dampen…or the way he towered over her to pull her into his arms would simply make her melt. There was a time when his back, that now always seemed to face her, was an edifice of muscular ridges to be honored with a touch…revered for the sheer pleasure of indulgence alone. And there was a time when his fingers trembled as they brushed her skin. There was also a time when they talked about his business, and her community work—which led to dreaming, which led to lovemaking, and hoping they were pregnant.

But that was almost six months ago…After waiting until she was almost forty to marry…after getting her education and shoring up her career, and foregoing babies…after choosing so wisely and so precisely on a mate…All of that gave way to constant arguments about bills, responsibilities, personal space…No one could have prepared her for this—not even Nana. Even that sage, with her parables dropped between the creation of biscuits and gravy, was gone.

During the weeks that had followed Nana's funeral, she'd told herself not to be sad, carefully reminding herself that her grandmother had led a full life, had died calmly of natural causes in her sleep, and had lived to the ripe old age of eighty-seven. Colette repeated this mantra as she flushed the toilet, washed her hands, and turned on the shower without turning on the light—peering briefly in the mirror, then deciding that it was too early to look at her own reflection in stark florescent.

The warm, steady pelt of water soothed the tight muscles in her neck, and she stretched and rolled her head from side to side, trying to stave off the heated sensations that had collected between her legs. What had happened to her grandmother was normal, to be expected. But the new distance between her and Franklin was not. It was an ache that lingered, like incomplete lovemaking.

As she turned herself to face the shower jet, its rhythmic pulse sent another wave of memory through her body. It had been so long since he'd touched her the way the water now caressed her skin, making her nipples rise and sting for attention. She brought her hands to her breasts and cupped them, kneading each hard, tiny pebble between her forefingers and thumbs. There was only one bathroom in the house down in Mystic Ridge, Maryland, and the house would be filled with her sister, her brother, his wife, her cousin, Wilton, and his pregnant wife, plus her cousin, Bey, and his trifling self…and, of course, Franklin…for a whole week. Feeling like this. Needing a release. With no private space to find it. She closed her eyes.

Her fingers worked against the angry flesh, gently rubbing the smooth surface of each globe in her hand, then reveling in the change of texture at each tip. As a shudder added a new source of moist warmth between her legs, she allowed the water to replace Franklin's kisses along her neck, slowly sliding her hands down to her lower belly and stopping to caress where they'd both hoped a baby would reside. She wasn't ready. Her hands returned a slow trail up her body. That's what he couldn't seem to remember. It took time to make love to a woman.

Foreplay started in the morning with a pleasant kiss, and a caring gesture, like bringing a cup of coffee up to bed to wake one's lover, followed by light conversation, and a deep kiss goodbye as they each went off to work. The dull ache within her had now turned into a throb, but she kept her hands moving in a slow circle around her breasts as she reminded her skin how lovemaking was supposed to be done.

She reached out and turned up the hot water, and reduced the coolness, then returned her hands to her belly. That was how it was supposed to be—anticipation created throughout the day. A telephone call to the job, just to say, "I love you." A little note slipped into a brown-bag. lunch, with an appointment for a home-bath-date hastily scribbled. Her inner thighs burned with repressed need as she parted them to allow the water entrance followed by her palms. She forced herself to be patient to make the desire grow, and abandoned her skin to lather her hands with soap.

Massaging the tender surface of the areas she'd already given attention, she dropped her head into the spray to drown out the sound of street traffic. Yes, that was how it was supposed to be…patient. After a kiss hello, and solid conversation about one's day. Making dinner together, with jazz on in the background, and removing the dishes while talking, waiting, and wondering when the right opportunity would present itself for touch.

Her fingers slid to the outer delicate folds that had now become so swollen that they opened on their own for affection. Then, she mentally whispered, they would curl up on the sofa by candle light with glasses of wine, and relax, holding each other, making plans for the future, dreaming. Her fingers kept time with the water, occasionally grazing the tiny bud of skin that now peeked through the pouting flower as they moved back and forth.

Another shudder made her wince with pleasure when she withdrew from the attention-starved nub, and gave affection to the aching areas around it. Time, it took time, to sit on the sofa and dream...and to let one's hand slide down an arm, then a hip, and to land well-placed kisses down a neck. It took time to gather a lover up into one's arms, and to whisper your deepest dreams. It took time to touch all the places they wanted you to touch, and to avoid all the places they desperately needed you to touch. It took time to slowly remove layers of clothes, one by one, and to land kisses behind every shred of cloth on each section of exposed skin. And, Lord, it took time to have your mouth revere their body in ways your hands could not. Only after that would they be ready.

Her fingers found a deep well and entered, then retreated to pay staccato homage to the ignored and angry bud, while her other hand found its way back up to her breasts, which were now throbbing and jealous. The final shudder that wracked her forced her to lean against the cool tile for a moment, and she stifled the moan that tried to pry its way up from her abdomen. Why couldn't Franklin understand that?

Tears blurred her vision as she hastily soaped and rinsed, then stepped out of the shower. This time when she looked in the mirror, she lingered. The unfocused image of herself became a space in time when one broke beans on the porch, or helped peel apples for the endless array of pies needed at the church, or one simply stirred the iced-tea as the wise woman chef responded with a textured phrase from a hymn.

She had planned to use her time at Mystic Ridge to gain much-needed knowledge, but time had run out. She was going to ask Nana how to rekindle a dying flame, how to stay married to the same man for fifty years, and how to make her body respond to him the way it once had—all the while knowing that she could ask these questions with a single sigh, and that question would be addressed in an answer without direct words from a sage that had become an accomplished telepath within her eighty-seven years of reading between the lines.

Instead, she'd only be going home to a horde of greedy cousins, siblings, and irritating spouses of siblings—there only with the intent to scavenge what they could from the dead, and to put the family's only true homestead on the market. The family peacekeeper was gone, and the one who had the wisdom, fortitude, and magic to bring all of these disparate tribes together, in peace, had gone Home herself.

It was almost too painful to fathom, as she brought a cold splash of water to her face and shook off the feeling of dread. Nana would have been the only person alive that could have repaired what was going so wrong with her and Franklin. There was no sense dwelling on it. She released another sigh and began brushing her teeth.

—⁓—

He'd become accustomed to awaking to an empty space on her side of the bed, just as he was getting used to the way she responded to him by rote— without true passion, or tenderness, anymore. This was not the way he'd envisioned spending the rest of his life, or their first Christmas together. Why couldn't they wait until January to go through Nana Johnson's things, and to put the house on the market? They already had everything.

Franklin pulled himself upright, and threw his legs over the side of the bed, and tried to shake the morning chill that crept up his shins and into his mind. What if Colette was really like them, the rest of her bourgeois family—down deep, and her independent, down-to-earth vibe was really just a lure to get him hooked? The only reason he'd agreed to this mess during his busy season was because of his love for Nana Johnson!

He could hear Colette washing up, and hesitated, remembering that there was a time when he would have slipped into the shower with her…just like there was a time when she couldn't get enough of him. Now, there were boundaries. Now, there were limitations. And, now, he was quite sure that, his wife had touched herself again this morning to complete her pleasure, instead of him…Just the way he had to, since the word "No" flowed from her lips more often than a "Yes."

Franklin listened and waited until the water in the sink stopped. Again, after they'd made love, she'd gotten up and had taken an unusually long time in the bathroom—alone. He'd heard the sound of the lock click, then the shower go on, then the rush of water stop after a while. It was a new sound that was becoming oddly familiar, one that he just couldn't get used to.

But, in truth, this morning was a pattern, like a timing belt that had gone wrong in an engine. The reality felt like cinder blocks had landed on his shoulders as he stood slowly and approached the door. He closed his eyes and thought of her lean cinnamon skin and petite breasts, with their darker brown nipples that no longer became erect for his touch…her short, thick auburn curls that called to his fingers, and her deep brown eyes that always looked sad these days. He wanted to hold her again, and to ask her what was wrong, beyond losing Nana—but the door was locked.

After waiting until he was damn near forty to marry, he'd imagined it to be different than his home-boys had warned. But it wasn't.

CHAPTER TWO

She watched him from the corner of her eye as their massive black four-by-four pulled onto Route 13 in Delaware. No matter what he said, and what they'd agreed upon, this was his car. Why that was so important to her now, she hadn't a clue. She only wished that she didn't have to leave Philadelphia to travel back home for this reason.

Oddly, her mind drifted in and out of the little vignettes of their morning conversation, and now the vehicle reminded her too much of Franklin. Black, dependable, silent...with a soft interior and strong motor, crooning jazz, and warm.

The previous forty-five minutes of interminable silence was wearing on her, but she decided not to let it show. Even his selection of jazz CDs was getting on her nerves, and his quiet civility made her want to scream. He had everything he wanted, it seemed— even down to their choice of what to listen to on the drive down to Nana's.

"Well, looks like the weather will hold till we get down there," she offered as a mild transition to a deeper conversation.

"Yup. If it's this clear on the way home, then it's all good."

She just looked at him briefly then focused her attention on the clear blue sky.

"Glad we got an early start before the traffic picked up."

"Uhm, hum."

"I think we'll get to the house first, and that way, we can settle in, choose the room we want, and get situated before the drama kings and queens arrive."

She did notice that a slight smile had formed at the corner of his mouth. She liked his mouth.

"Like I said, it's all good, baby."

"Is that all you can say?"

For the first time since they'd entered the car, he looked over at her for moment then returned his attention to the road. He knew that a conflict was probable this morning, and had been trying his best to avoid one. It was all in the way she got dressed, literally snatching on her clothes, and in the way she gave him one-word responses over breakfast, and snapped off orders and details about how much and what to pack. He could feel it, sense it was on its way—just like birds take cover for a pending rain storm long before people even notice the winds have picked up.

"Tell me, during what part of this conversation was I supposed to say something more?"

"Don't patronize me," she whispered.

Okay, it was on.

He'd put forth the question without looking at her, and her answer came with a soft click of annoyance as she sucked her teeth and huddled herself more closely against the passenger's door. He knew the sound. It was the response that black women offer when truly disgusted.

More silence. Five more miles of silence. Maybe she'd let it go.

"It's just that, you never have anything to say anymore."

He knew the drill. She wasn't going to let it go. That left two options. Either get it all out and try to resolve it before they got to the house, or he could leave it be, and drive in peace. But then he'd have to try to resolve whatever it was after they got there, and after everybody else got there. Fighting in Mom Johnson's house, with her family reinforcements present, was out of the question.

"What do you mean I don't have anything to say any more? We talk."

He watched her from the corner of his eye. After a moment of apparent contemplation, she seemed to relax and turn her body more in his direction. Oh, yeah, this was going to be a long one.

"No, Franklin, we don't."

"I don't get it. It's not like I don't say good morning…or like I don't—"

"—You don't say good morning like you used to." His mind searched for any shred of logic that could be salvaged. "What's that supposed to mean?"

"See, now you're getting defensive, which is why we can never talk about what we need to talk about."

He let out his breath slowly, and tried to remain calm.

"Look, I know you miss your grandmother. So do I. She was a lovely woman. I also know how much you don't want to be going down to the house, right before Christmas to pack up her things, but they over-ruled your vote, and mine, so we have to go. I can't imagine having to deal with this, especially after losing your Mom and Dad five years ago to cancer and a heart attack. And, maybe I didn't want to talk about it, because I knew you had to be hurt to the bone. Truthfully, I haven't quite known what to say to you about any of it."

"That's not the issue, and that's not what I'm talking about and you know it. We've been over that already."

When she let out a long sigh, he extended his arm across her shoulders and held the steering wheel with one hand. "Listen, I know it's still bothering you, no matter what you say. That's why I'm here. I gotchure back. Okay? Me and you. We'll deal with your people the same way we've gotta deal with mine, with a long-handled spoon, as my grandmother would say. Then, we'll come home and make Christmas for just the two of us."

He noticed that her eyes were glistening when she leaned against his shoulder.

"But I've dealt with losing Mom and Dad, you know. Mom was the hard one, because we didn't expect the cancer, and it came on her and took her so fast...Dad's heart attack was almost a blessing for him. He loved her so much."

"Yeah," he offered quietly, "but, sometimes, one thing has a way of triggering a memory about something else. You know?"

"Maybe," she nearly whispered, "but Nana was eighty-seven, and wasn't even sick. So, when she passed in her sleep, we all knew it was time."

"True, but, it still don't take away all the hurt."

"I know," she said in a soft voice, "but it still doesn't answer why we've been having problems for the last six months. Nana wasn't sick when this marriage started unraveling."

He had no answer to that, nor had he expected such an honest statement of fact.

"I don't know, baby. Maybe relationships just have an ebb and flow? For a while, we was flowin' pretty good; then we had a little ebb...and that low tide ran right into this situation making everything feel dried out. Now, it's hard to tell what has you down."

"It's not just me, Franklin. We're both going through something."

Again, he had no answer. She was digging deep this morning. He allowed the road to consume him as he pondered what she'd just said.

They rode for miles in companionable silence, her head resting on his shoulder. He was glad that she didn't appear hostile and withdrawn, but he hated the sadness that enveloped her. When he pulled off the main highway onto the narrow two-lane divide, he looked at the barren trees and bleak ice-covered hills that had once been lush and green and full of life. The truth was everything had its own season...but that didn't make winter any easier to endure.

—⁓—

The single lane road that they turned onto was icy, but it was passable. The branches of the trees hung heavy within a clear crystalline casing, laden from their burden, and seeming to bow as their four-by-four passed them. Deep, frozen tire ruts within stiff mud made Franklin withdraw his arm from her shoulder and hold the steering wheel with both hands. The change in sensation allowed a renewed chill to seep into her bones.

Small farmhouses dotted the landscape, each sitting back from the main road like silent observers protected from encroachment by wide front yards and fields. It was so peaceful, motionless, where the absolute quiet almost forbade one to speak.

Nana's house soon came into plain view. Colette's stomach lurched. It was just as she'd last seen it only a few weeks ago. But it was so still. It was also covered with a delicate coating of ice that created a spectacular prism of light which appeared to bounce from the surfaces. Almost as if the entire house had been wrapped and sealed in cellophane, and put away for something special, she thought, wondering how beautiful it would be in Mystic Ridge if it ever snowed.

Yes…for the moment, home was still there. The large bay window stood watch over the wooden porch that rimmed the property, with yellow shutters winking a welcome to all visitors. Wide wooden steps formed an apron against the long dirt path, framed by two fenced-in vegetable gardens that now lay fallow under winter. Everything was the same—except the fact that Nana wasn't on the porch to look down the lane and wave. Now, a sparkling icy blanket of silence replaced her smile and made the house vacant.

"You think I should pull up in front of the shed, or the barn?"

Colette shrugged and sighed. The front path to the house had been salted, as well as the driveways leading to both structures—no doubt, courtesy of the members of the church, and Miss Julia's son, Juney's, home training. "Closer would be better, I suppose."

Without a response, Franklin pulled the vehicle to a stop in front of the large outdoor tool shed, pushed the back-hatch button, and hopped out. Colette kept her gaze on the house, then exited the vehicle with another sigh, and headed up the path after she'd grabbed her garment bag. It took a moment to find the keys in the bottom of her large satchel purse, and he took her luggage so she could dig for them.

"Looks like everything is in order," Franklin murmured, as they entered the large sun-lit foyer and closed the door behind them.

Colette nodded, and allowed her gaze to scan the spacious rooms that faced her. Everything was in order. Too much order. The brightly colored hook rug under their feet seemed newly vacuumed, and each of her grandmother's hand-made, needlepoint pillows in the living room was in its place, resting in the corners of the two overstuffed armchairs by the fireplace. Clean, crisp doilies frocked the plump, floral sofa, and the floors and wooden mantle glistened with a coat of fresh furniture polish. Stained glass sun-catchers merrily spilled colored prisms along the adjacent walls, and her line of vision scanned for the merest hint of unwanted intrusion. Relief swept through her when she spied the row of silver-framed pictures on the mantle. Those were the true house treasures, each one bearing an irreplaceable moment in time captured on yellowing celluloid.

"I think everything is okay, Colette."

He watched her shoulders drop an inch before she spoke.

"So pretty…and such a shame that it's going out of the family. I hate the fact that people were in here from the church after we left, to clean it."

"I just think folks was trying to help, and to do a little something nice, is all—like the way they did the driveways for us. I don't think nobody meant no harm, honey. They all loved Ester, and this was all they could do to show their respects. C'mon. Tell me which room you want us to be in, and I'll put the bags up there."

"I want to check the dining room and kitchen, first."

He didn't argue with her—that she appreciated. He also didn't follow her. That, too, she appreciated.

Without looking back, she crossed the living room and went into the dining area. Her eyes settled on the large oak ellipse of a table and matching spoke chairs that were handmade by her grandfather's patient craft. She touched one of the needlepoint seat cushions, and smiled, remembering the fuss Nana always made when they'd accidentally spill something on them as children.

Each dish, and rows of crystal stemware, were still arranged museum-style behind the beveled glass of her grandfather's family-famous breakfront, with large serving platters displayed prominently in plate-holders across the top. Her fingers slid across the ivory crocheted tablecloth that her mother had given Nana as an anniversary present. It had taken her mother so long to finish it, so many years ago, and the Tiffany lamp still added a splash of color to the pale yellows and blues in the room...it was a gift from her brother, one that Nana cherished. "She loved that, Wilton," Colette whispered, "Glad she and Pop got to enjoy it." She ignored the ostentatious chandelier that Bey had competitively added to the room the following year.

Moving into the kitchen, and flicking the overhead light on, Colette stood in the middle of what had once seemed like Grand Central Station. She remembered teaming with her sister to replace the old linoleum table with a genuine butcher block one and low oak stools that now took center stage. Her cousins had replaced the cutlery that was now motionless. But nobody, not even her father, could get Nana to part with her cast-iron skillets. The best they'd been able to do was to buy her a suitable rack upon which to retrieve and store her magic pots.

How many meals, she wondered, had been prepared at that six-foot wooden room divider? Biscuits, and breads, and green beans, and stews, and chickens had even been beheaded there. Iced-tea, and fresh lemonade had been squeezed, as local and family gossip got poured into pitchers along with the seeds and sugar.

This was the real family room, not the living room. Colette allowed her gaze to travel to the refrigerator, and she suddenly stopped. A note with an elderly scrawl made her do a double take and catch her breath. That wasn't there before, when they'd come down for the funeral. But she relaxed as she approached it. The note was simplistic, and the message clear.

We washed up the linens for you, baby. Refrigerator is cleaned out, save some fresh eggs and milk for breakfast. You know our Ester, jams and mason vegetables been put up since early Fall, and God bless her, her pantry was full when she passed. You young folk don't need to go to the market for nothing much—you family, love you like my own. Come see me when you get settled in. I got mail from the house, as Mr. Whitfield brings it to me now like Ester told him to. —Love, Miss Julie

Colette stood there for a moment, and fought back the tears. Exiting the kitchen quietly, she clicked off the light and joined Franklin at the bottom of the staircase.

Accepting his gentle lead, she headed up the steps, glad that they had been the first to arrive. As they reached the top of the landing, she hesitated not knowing which direction to turn.

To her left was her grandparents' bedroom. She definitely didn't want to sleep in there, even with Franklin beside her, and despite the fact that it was one of the closest rooms to the bathroom.

"Let me walk the halls a bit by myself, okay?"

Franklin set the bags down and waited. At the moment, she appreciated his silent acquiescence. She knew he understood her need to drink in the pure quiet, with only the large grandfather clock in the hall ticking. This space had never been so still, not even during the funeral. And there would never be another opportunity like this again.

Colette walked down the hallway alone, leaving Franklin where he stood. She poked her head into what had been her grandparents' room, first. The neat four-posted bed sat high off the floor and donned a pristine set of lemon-yellow linen beneath the same clean, white quilt with doves and white roses on it that had been in her Nana's wedding trousseau.

Mending that quilt had been an ongoing labor of love for her grandmother for years. Now, looking at it with new eyes, she finally understood why. That's where they'd probably talked. That's where they'd shared secrets. That's where they'd made enough love to produce three wonderful children. That's the place in the house where her grandmother and grandfather had probably formed their life's dreams…where intimacy and warmth privately resided…and that's why her grandmother could never part with her new-bride's quilt, no matter how tattered and frayed it became. It was a shrine of memories, lovingly repaired every season by a woman who remembered.

The vanity had also withstood the test of time, and still held her grandmother's silver comb and brush set—another wedding present from a lifetime of love.

"She used to brush our hair with that when we were little," Colette whispered to herself, her eyes filling with unshed tears. Then she turned away.

It was clear that whoever had come in to clean had been honest and diligent to a flaw. What had been wrong with her for begrudging those loving hands a last connection to Nana? She'd been living in the city too long, and infested with its twisted values. Ester Johnson was a community treasure, to be shared by all, and missed by all. Colette drew another slow breath and relaxed.

The entire house almost looked as if Nana Johnson had carefully cleaned everything herself. Someone had even taken down and washed the yellow and white dotted Swiss curtains at the windows, and dusted the end tables, and dutifully returned the family Bible to its familiar perch on the night-stand by the bed on a doily. Her brother and his wife were older, had been married the longest, and deserved to be here, she thought, mentally arranging things as she walked.

She made her way down the hall and peered into her uncles' rooms. The same neat, tidy appearance of order faced her, and the twin beds made her smile. She and her sister used to share that room during their summers in the country, happily bouncing from bed to bed until Nana hollered at them to stop. Yes, it wouldn't be hard to convince her sister to take this room at all. She now wondered why they'd all chosen to stay at a motel in the center of town for those three days of the funeral, instead of coming home?

As she approached her father's room, she drew another steadying breath. He was gone too, just like her mother, but the neat little room was cozy, and had a queen-sized bed and a broad window with a cushioned window-seat and large armchair. It was perfect for Wilton and Deidre. She did need her rest, being eight months pregnant, and everything. The large feather bed would make her comfortable...plus, it was directly across the hall from the bathroom—which would be a definite asset. It was probably good that her father was the eldest son, and therefore had been given the best room in the house, second to Nana and Pop's. At least, there was an extra couple-comfortable room, so no unnecessary squabbles would occur on that issue, anyway.

Colette slipped into the last room, and just as she'd expected, the bathroom was spotless. The white claw-footed tub and porcelain sink sparkled with an old-fashioned brand of elbow grease. The sight almost made her weep with gratitude, and it took the last edge off her misgivings about other people intruding.

She touched the edges of the silver frames that graced the hall as she made her way back to Franklin's side, adjusting pictures ever so slightly, and relaxing, finding the old rhythms of Southern easy speech and a slower gait, simply remembering as her fingers grazed them.

"Everything all right?" he murmured when she reached him.

"Yeah," she whispered, going ahead of him toward the other end of the second floor. "There's nothing to do to get ready for the others. Every room has been done. I need to go by Miss Julie's house and thank her personally when 1 get Nana's mail."

"You know where you want us to be?" he asked in a quiet tone before picking up the bags, still reverent of her mood.

"I'm gonna put Wilton and Deidre in Daddy's old room, Brother and Nancy in Nana's—that's only right, he's the oldest. Nicole can go in the room we used to share as kids, since she'll be the only one sleeping alone up here, and knowing my sister, she'll be trying to jump into bed with us if something goes bump in the night."

Franklin chuckled, and for the first time that day, she joined him.

"Now, you know, that'll put Beynard next to us, if we take the extension and he and his lady take Pop Johnson's little reading room."

"Yeah, I know," she sighed. "But I like Nana's sewing room. Pop built it for her with his own hands...and they put a big daybed in there, with windows all around...a comfy chair...and he even put his tiny room beside it so they could talk without him getting in her way." A small chuckle at the thought surprised her, and she smiled as she remembered how her grandmother and grandfather lovingly and constantly fussed at each other in an age-old repartee. "He even made her a full length floor-mirror, so she could let her clients see her handiwork and do gown fittings. He really, really loved her."

"A lotta love went into all of this house," Franklin said in earnest from his vantage point behind her close to the room, all the while appreciating the craftsmanship that had gone into the exposed beams and hand-hung windowpanes. "Always admired your grandpop. Was a true artisan. Don't teach cabinet-making and carpentry to them young boys, like they used to. Everything was done by hand, no fancy machines."

"He built the extension for her because she always wanted the boys' rooms to be intact for when they came home with their wives and kids...guess he got

tired of sitting on her pins in the living room furniture," she chuckled again sadly. "She never got used to
any of her children being gone. Guess I'll know what
that feels like one day." Before Franklin could
comment, she turned away from him and paced
toward the room. "It gets all the light, and at night,
the stars and trees look so beautiful. And she made
every curtain, and pillow, and bedspread in here
herself, too. This room has both of them in
it…laughing and talking, with a door in-between, and
one to enter from the hall, if they needed individual
space. I love this new little nook they created."

"You don't have to sell me," he whispered,
catching up to her and landing a kiss against her neck
as they moved deeper into the room. "It's just that Bey
keeps strange hours, and might keep you up with his
hootin' and loud talkin'."

She turned and considered the comment, then
walked over to the small room that hosted a pull-out
sofa, desk, bookshelves, and wooden chair, and looked
in. "If trifling-ass Bey brings that same floozie to this
house again, and screws her under Nana's roof while
we're trying to deal with serious business, like he did
during the funeral, I'll kick his natural behind. I'm
not havin' it! I will not keep quiet this time! Why, I'll
unlock that damned door and turn on the light,
and—"

"—Slow down, slow down, baby," Franklin urged
with a smile. "Now, the man is grown, and has a right

to have his lady friend join him, and it ain't our business what they—"

"—Oh, so, now, you're taking his side!"

Franklin set his load of bags down very carefully and walked over to the adjoining room door, closed it, and threw the latch. "Why don't you just put Sissey in there?"

"Because, Sissey shouldn't have to be put out of what's familiar to her just because Bey's a pig!"

"Well, everybody mourns a little different, honey. Bey just got tore up the day before the funeral, and grieved in some flesh…you can't hold a man hostage for—"

"—What!"

"All I'm saying is…" Franklin stifled a smile, let the comment trail off, and began arranging the bags neatly at the foot of the daybed.

"Oh, and I suppose you have the same intentions while we're here? Well, forget it. This is Nana's house!"

"Now, don't jump to conclusions, and go killin' the messenger. I just think once everyone is here, and we get to workin', we should all let bygones be bygones. I brought my tools, and I'll fix anything that's out of order…noticed the mailbox was leaning a bit. I'll get on that this afternoon. Will walk the perimeter and see if there's anything that could hurt the selling price, and fix it, okay? That's my contribution, and all I'ma say—for now."

Franklin gave her an impish grin, then walked toward the door. The man truly got on her nerves!

CHAPTER THREE

He hadn't been able to pry Colette out of the house all morning, not even to stop in on Miss Julia to pay her respects. She seemed determined to set out towels on the foot of each bed, and to thaw out meats and greens for dinner, and determined most of all to be the first presence in the house everyone else encountered when they arrived. It was some sort of weird female squatter's rights ritual, if not a territorial marking ceremony—the way she took absolute physical possession of the kitchen. But, the house was still going on the market within the week. It had been decided. So her attempt was futile, and sure to only get the feathers flying around there. Besides, what was the point? Pure crazy. At least that's what it seemed like to his way of looking at it; however, even that rational argument didn't change things. The woman would not be moved.

His retreat had been to go outside and work on straightening the leaning mailbox post. It was a safer distance than standing idly by, chatting with a half-angry, half-crying woman. And there was definitely no reasoning with her.

"How do? Looks like you workin' mighty hard on that post."

Solomon Whitfield's voice startled him, and Franklin pulled his head up quickly, then relaxed and smiled as he squinted in the afternoon sun to make out the local postman's face.

"Yo! Mr. Whitfield, how you be?"

"Jus' fine, son. Jus' fine. No aches, pains, no complains. But was, and still am, sorry to hear about Miz Ester. Beautiful lady. Everybody's gonna miss her."

Franklin pulled off his baseball cap and wiped his brow with the forearm portion of his down jacket. Even though it was cold outside, the exertion of digging up the post from the frozen earth was beginning to take its toll. He leaned back on the fence and nodded in agreement with Mr. Whitfield. He liked talking to a fellow Southerner. It relaxed his tongue, and his mind, as he could easily slip into the comfortable dialect without feeling any sense of being on-guard the way he normally did around Colette's family.

"You ain't said a mumblin' word, brother." He allowed each syllable to escape in a slow, patient drawl. "I'm just fixin' a few things, and trying to stay outta harm's way until the rest of the family gets down here."

Whitfield adjusted the mailbag on his shoulder, and shook his head in a gesture of understanding;

then he cast his line of vision down the road in the direction of Miss Julia's house.

"Yeah, I imagine Colette took it the worse, which means, you gonna have to weather the worse, sorry to say."

A companionable silence enveloped them, and Franklin let his breath out slowly.

"Her brother, Girard, should be here soon, which'll be good," Franklin offered after a moment. "He's the executor, and the family attorney. Good people, fair people, so...I know he'll handle things the way Mom Johnson wanted. That oughta take some'a the load off of Colette."

"Hmmm...maybe," Whitfield mumbled, rubbing his chin and squinting at the late afternoon sky. "You know, Ester never wanted this house to be sold to no developers. Wanted it kept in the family."

Again, all Franklin could do for a moment was shake his head in agreement. "Yup, but that ain't my call, man. I'm just the hired help," he added with a sad chuckle. "Right shame, too. This place is like something people dream of...but all of 'em couldn't make it a week in here together, so I guess Girard is gonna do the only rational thing. Sell it, split the proceeds, and move on."

The statement seemed to take the conversation out of Solomon Whitfield for a moment. He just leaned against the fence with Franklin and looked down the road in the same direction. After a while, he pushed himself away from the leaning white pickets and adjusted his mailbag again.

"You know, this house has been in the Johnson family since just after slavery. One of the last Negro strongholds in this tiny town of nobodies. History. Why, the folks that held onto this house saw two World Wars, The Great Depression, Jim Crow…buried kin in the family plot out back, and raised generations here."

"Sir," Franklin offered quietly, "you preaching to the choir. My Colette has been like a Wild West pioneer about the decision, since she heard it…wouldn't be surprised if she stood on the porch with a rifle and dared the revenuers to come on her land."

"Don't laugh," Whitfield chuckled, "I saw old man Johnson chase off a sheriff from the next town over, one time, just like that—rifle in hand, back in the Klan riding days.

"Yeah, well, it might come to that in here this week."

"That bad, really?"

"Really," Franklin sighed, straightening himself away from the fence, and to get closer to Whitfield's good ear. "Got bad about six months ago. We'd come down for a visit, and Mom Johnson was moving slower than normal. Was showing Colette who was to get what in the house, and singing hymns more than usual. Told Colette that even though Brother Girard had the solid mind, Colette had the fairer heart.

Scared my poor wife to death. She said it was a sign. When we got home, Colette cried and cried like a baby, and there was no talkin' to her, neither. I couldn't do nothin' about the way she felt, and all she kept telling me was, time was short. So I started working crazy hours, trying to make my auto-body business rake in enough to possibly buy the house—if said dark hour ever came. But then we started fighting about money and bills…'cause I stopped taking her out and stuff…was trying to hold onto every penny, though I never told her why. I mean, we argued about who was to do what in the house—stupid stuff…I was so tired, and takin' on too many body-jobs to help out and make things easier, like I used to…and I sorta lost interest in the day to day things, if'n you know what I mean."

Franklin cast his gaze to the ground, and for the first time, his admission felt like a heavy burden had been lifted from his shoulders. Whitfield's reassuring slap across his back made him feel better.

"You tell your wife any of this?"

"You crazy?" Franklin muttered, shaking his head no. "Look, I waited till I was damned near forty to marry her…watched her lose both her Mom and her Dad, then her Grandpop, before I could get myself together to give her a date to go along with the ring. Engaged the woman for five and a half years…Hell, her brother had to be the one to walk her down the dag-gone aisle…all the while, I was claiming that I wouldn't be ready to make things official until I got my business together. Stupid! Short-sighted."

"Don't be too hard on yourself, son—"

"—No. Truth is naked truth. 'Cause, then, when I finally did marry her, all I can do is put her in a row house. Sure, I make a decent livin' now, but it still ain't enough to cover what we dreamed about. What I promised her our life would be. You understand?"

"Dreams gotsta be pursued together. It ain't all on the one. I know if Ester Johnson was here right now, she'd tell you that much."

"Yeah, but I'm still the man of the house. The weight's on me."

Whitfield placed his hand on Franklin's shoulder and looked him straight in the eyes. "If I know our Colette, and I been knowin' her ever since she was in her mother's belly, she wouldn't hold you responsible for tryin' as hard as you did—no matter what the outcome. In fact, she'd love you even more because you even cared to try."

Franklin pulled away and sought the fence to lean on again. "Tryin' don't cut it, no offense, Mr. Whitfield. I didn't produce. She got men in her family that can put their money where their mouth is, and that's what they'll be doin' when they come down here today. I can't say diddly on the subject of what happens. All I can do is hold her hand as they run her out of town on a rail and let her take a few boxes."

"Her grandpop didn't have nothin' when he and Miz Ester started, and—"

"—Not to cut you off, or to get philosophical, but she's used to men in her family that have achieved something of note. Grandpop Johnson started out as a furniture-maker, and built his business to the point where he made this house into a national treasure…you should see the work that man put into his home. Like something I always dreamed of doing for my family one day—never could stand the city life," he added on an exhale. "Always wanted to go back south, home."

"You can't compare yourself to a man that had no other options. In Pops Johnson's day, a black man had to work for hisself, or die tryin', and that seems to be whatchure doin' in Philadelphia. Right? A woman can't ask for more than that. Can't get blood from no turnip. I seen ya, and Ester done tol' me plenty times, you work hard, boy. She was proudest of you…said you reminded her so much of her husband, Ezekiel."

"No excuses, Mr. Whitfield. The fact is, the next generation did okay for themselve. Got a solid education and good jobs. Me, I went into the service, then went to vo-tech school. Stupid. Colette's brother's a lawyer, a big time lawyer."

"He ain't do that by hisself. Ester scrubbed floors to send her son, his Dad, to Morehouse College. And, her brother, Girard, missed Vietnam by the skin of his chinny-chin-chin—Ester's prayers being heard On High, no doubt. And he only went to law school 'cause his grandmother encouraged him to fight for Civil Rights—now, what he did with that degree ain't have nothin' to do with what Ester originally intended. That much, I do know."

Franklin ignored Solomon Whitfield's argument, and pressed on. "Even her Dad was an engineer, at Boeing, back in the day—"

"All 'cause he was in the right place at the right time after a lawsuit, which is why Ester was so high on law for Girard. Law got his daddy into Boeing. Civil Rights."

Not to be dissuaded, Franklin continued without missing a beat as he ticked off the lineage on his fingers. "Her cousin, Wilton, has some muck-t-muck post down at Hampton University—"

"—Cause he married the right girl at the right time, whose family was in the Virginia upper crust Negro society."

"—Even triflin' Bey is a dentist."

"Now, you got me there. That's still one of the eighth wonders of the world!" Solomon Whitfield slapped his knee and laughed at his own joke, and poked Franklin in the chest when he couldn't even get him to chuckle. "Aw, c'mon, son. Life's too short to be woulda, coulda, shoulda-ing. You never know what's gonna happen. Ester was the one who always said, it's a long road that has no turn."

Still caught up in his own litany, Franklin let out a breath and watched it turn to steam. "Why Colette picked me, out of all her choices, only God knows. Shoot. The woman can't even quit her job and do her grants to start that community center she dreamed about. She needs to get out of that dead-end city job at DHS, people with problems too serious to solve day in, day out. And too much bureaucracy to help 'em. All the girl really ever wanted to do was work with kids, under her own terms, and teach 'em basic stuff like Ester Johnson taught them."

Franklin held up his hand to stop Mr. Whitfield from defending him further. "What's worse is, truth be told, Mr. Whitfield—since we speakin' man to man. I couldn't even do the easiest thing, and the simplest thing, she wanted…then, I'd have to tell her that I couldn't even save her grandma's house. Nah…no use in tellin' her about failing one more stupid dream."

The postman looked at him hard now, and set down his bag. "What's the simplest thing?"

"I don't even need to be bothering you with this nonsense. You a working man, got letters to deliver, and it's ass-biting cold out here." Franklin turned his back to Solomon Whitfield and lunged at the stubborn post that refused to budge.

"You know, stress'll make a lot of things stop workin' the way dey normally would. Now, I maybe an ole country boy…but, I hear tell your people is from North Carolina good stock. Blessin's will come to you soon, son, in God's time. But, in the meantime, y'all needta get Miss Julia to give you some a her medicinals, and have a talk with your wife about how you been feelin'. All dat stress ain't good to keep bottled up. Gotta release it, and let go and let God.

Young folk can die of heart attacks too, ya know. Dreams is good medicine—goes along with prayers, but you gotta share 'em for it to work."

Although Franklin kept working at the post without turning around, half talking to himself as he did so, he grunted out a question-part-statement to Solomon Whitfield that was so quiet, he was sure the old man didn't hear it.

"When Wilton's very pregnant wife gets down here, all Hell is gonna break lose on-top of everything else, and if," he added with a pant of exertion as he took a second lunge at the post, "Miss Julie got some magic in her kitchen, I'd be much obliged."

He heard the postman's bag lift, and when he finally looked up, Solomon Whitfield was on his way down the road heading for Miss Julia's house.

—⁓—

The sound of a large sedan pulling into the driveway brought her to the kitchen window. Her brother Girard's gleaming black Mercedes seemed so out of place against the simple country backdrop of the front yard. She watched and nearly held her breath as her brother rounded the exterior of the vehicle and opened the door for her sister-in-law. Her jaw went slack as a sleek black mink-covered arm appeared first, and the always-elegant Nancy descended from her chariot.

"Well, it's on, now, Nana," she whispered into the open space. "The carpet-baggers are here to break your home up and box it away into a million pieces."

Colette wiped the flour from her hands onto her grandmother's apron. She'd be sure to lean in without bodily touching Nancy when she greeted her. The crunch of icy driveway brought her to the window again, only to see that a steel gray Volvo had pulled in next to the Mercedes. "All right. Wilton and Deidre got here," she sighed. Now all she had to do was wait for Bey to bring his red BMW careening into the yard. If she knew Nicole, she'd probably paid for a cab all the way from the airport.

As expected, Nancy had laced her arm around Franklin's waist, and it took both her brother and Franklin to haul in the assorted heavy Louis Vitton luggage while duly escorting Nancy up the steps. God forbid the queen should take a skid on the ice. Colette steadied her nerves and stood at the front screen door with a pasted-on smile, braving the cold and bracing for impact.

CHAPTER FOUR

Standing in the middle of the kitchen high-traffic zone, Colette wondered almost aloud, why it seemed that when Nana was alive, the same number of bodies in the same space would flow in a more orchestrated fashion. This was sheer chaos!

Somehow, her grandmother could seem to talk, and dispatch duties effectively and in accordance to skill levels, all the while never missing a beat. Now, however, the once-calm terrain seemed to be manned by an uninitiated and confused air-traffic controller—her.

Nancy, her sister-in-law, was swinging her immaculate jet-black bob hair-cut at every opportunity, and trying desperately not to chip a French-manicured fingernail, or to splash food on her Nile-blue silk dress. God forbid that any organic particle might get trapped in the setting of the four-karat rock her brother had given the woman, and Heaven forbid that she take off her Rolex watch to avoid getting it wet while making dinner. How in the Hell was she going to call herself helping in the kitchen with that get-up on? Colette had to admit that the woman looked good, athletically trim, no hint of gray, full-face makeup—beat down, always, upon flawless cappuccino skin. She had to admit it, even if begrudgingly so, that she didn't know a woman alive who exuded Nancy's level of elegance. But the heifer was in the way, nonetheless, and was always trying to Grand Stand.

Without thinking about it twice, Colette had simply reached in the drawer and handed Nancy a full apron, and a designated spot to be on the other side of the butcher's block, yet in the middle of the kitchen, which ended the circling and directing from Nancy—for the moment.

Colette knew she was getting tired, just by the way she was starting to answer people. She was almost ready to give her tall, stylish sister, Nicole, a shower cap to cover her short, curly blonde-brown ringlets—if she didn't stop playing with her hair and twisting it while preparing food! At least Nicole didn't require full hazmat covering, since her tie-dyed, New York chic outfit could get splashed, and no one would know the difference.

Even though Beynard's friend, Sandra, annoyed her with her constant coos and overtly sexual commentary thrown in Bey's direction, at least the young woman held to a basic standard of food prep cleanliness. In fact, Sandra was growing on her, even though she was only twenty-five and had everything hanging out in the dead of winter, she was much less of a pain than Wilton's wife, Deidre—who got in the way, whined, and complained at every turn. If Deidre would just sit her big, water-buffalo butt down!

Between Sandra's squeaky, cutesie voice emanating from her tiny coffee-colored, half-naked frame, Deidra's constant deer-in-the-headlights look of sheer confusion coming from her wide brown eyes, and her sister's know-it-all news-anchor voice competing with Nancy's too-bored-to-be-bothered-and-where's-the-maid approach to cooking a basic family dinner, Colette thought she'd pass out.

Finally, when a mid-air collision occurred between her sister, Nicole, and Bey's friend, Sandra, Colette held her hands out and stopped all motion.

"STOP! Freeze. Nobody move."

The bewildered members of the near pile-up laughed and screeched to a halt.

"Y'all, this don't make no sense," Colette chuckled. "Okay, Deidre , get your big self into that chair that your husband brought in, out of the way in the corner, and sit down like Wilton told you to. You can fold the napkins for dinner on what's left of your lap."

"Yes, Ma'am," Deidre giggled, and scurried into the corner and flopped down with a grunt that made everyone laugh even harder.

"Sissey, get on that high stool by the sink—no, not in front of the sink—you ain't at work at the news desk, and there's no cameras here. Sit to the side of it, so everybody can get to the water. Thank you, and make the iced tea. Everything you need is right there.

And, Sandra, I know this is your first time at this, but it's all about choreographed rhythm. Stay to your side of the butcher block next to Nancy—our resident expert, follow her lead, she's slicing what you peel, try not to cut her, and stay up on a stool while you're peeling those yams, and you won't cut your dang self."

Sandra laughed, and joined in with the rest of the giggles. "Bey!" she exclaimed, when Nicole slapped his wrist as he leaned over her to get to the sink, "Go get water for your scotch from up in the bathroom. Stop running in and out of here for stuff. That's how I almost wiped-out Nicole, trying to rinse off this knife and not bump into you!"

"That's right, Bey," Nancy chimed in. "It's bad enough that Wilton is sashaying in here every five minutes to check on his wife, and Girard and Franklin are hovering in the doorway like two yard dogs waiting for a scrap to fall…why don't you fellas just go somewhere?"

"You tell 'em, Nance," Colette added, popping the back of Franklin's knuckles with a wooden spoon as he tried to open her vat of greens for a peek. "Stop sweatin' the pots!"

"Dag, y'all are some mean women," Bey laughed amiably, then smoothed his fingers through his short, silky, salt and pepper hair. "I'm just adding to my cups. Why y'all so mean to old Bey—they treat me bad, Frank."

"Totally vicious," Franklin belly-laughed as he rubbed his knuckles and tried to avoid another whack from Colette's spoon. "Mom Johnson would let us come in and get a taste, but yall are just plain evil."

Nancy put one hand on her hip and brandished a flat skillet filled with warm butter in it with the other. "Mom Johnson ain't here to save your sorry butts. Now move it, and make yourselves useful by setting the table, at least."

"Dag, a man can't even get a little taste of hooch before dinner. What's the world coming to?" Bey added in an overly dramatic tone. He flashed Sandra a wide, perfect smile, and she giggled at the attention. "What we having for dinner, anyway…somethin' sure smells good."

"Colette was nice enough to get things started this morning when she got here. She made three apple pies, plus we got baked chicken, fried tomatoes, yams, greens, biscuits, potato salad, and iced tea. Satisfied? Now scram!" Deidre ordered with a laugh.

"Gentlemen, I say we retreat, now, while we have a fighting chance," Girard chimed in with a wide smile. "We're outnumbered and out-gunned, and they have sophisticated culinary weapons."

"But, I think it's too hot in here for Deidre," Wilton protested.

A collective groan echoed out from the group. It was enough of an indictment to make the other three men bodily carry Wilton away from his wife, and into the dining room.

"We got one wounded," Franklin laughed as they hoisted a wiggling, chubby Wilton up by his arms.

"I say we shoot him, and put him out of his misery," Bey laughed as they all struggled to get through the door arch at the same time.

"No, can't shoot him," Girard bellowed in a faux-military voice. "We're Marines, and we never leave our wounded behind."

As soon as the men had gotten to the other side of the doorway, all the women doubled-over and laughed. Nancy was the first one to salute Colette. The fact that her sister-in-law did so made Colette further disarm.

"Well defended, Captain Cole!" Nancy quipped with a grin, accidentally getting yam sugar on her forehead in the process. "Every station present and accounted for. I'd say we couldn't have done this better."

Each woman stood up a bit straighter, and then made a grimace to denote her intention to bravely protect her position in the kitchen, which brought another round of uproarious laughter.

"Lord have Mercy!" Deidre sighed, "I never thought we'd get rid of them!"

"Girl!" her sister, Nicole, huffed, "I don't see how you all stand it? That's why I'm still single."

"It's just like when we were kids, remember," Colette laughed, setting biscuits on a cookie sheet from her post. "Grandma had to have her hands full with that bunch under foot all the time."

"Oh, like the time when we were out back, hanging sheets for Nana, and crazy Bey and Girard were chasing poor Wilton with a dead field mouse. He came tearing around the corner, got tangled in the wet sheets, took out the entire clothes line, and we had to scrub all that yard-dirt outta Nana's linens—by hand. She was so mad at us, and all of us got a whippin' for messing up her laundry." Nicole, leaned back and roared with laughter at the memory.

"No!" Nancy, exclaimed. "Girard never told me that."

"Oh, girl," Colette added in, wiping her eyes with mirth, "my brother, your husband, was a terror. I'm sure there's plenty he didn't tell. Don't let that sedate façade of Mr. Attorney fool you. He tortured me and Nicole, all the time. Bey was his running buddy, and they would gang up on poor chubby little Wilton…me and Sissey used to feel sorry for that chile."

"Bey and Girard?" Nancy said in shock, but accepted the statement as both Nicole and Colette nodded in unison.

Deidre shook her head. "Now see, why'd they abuse my poor Wilton like that?"

"Cause he was a cry-baby butterball," Nicole chuckled, "and used to tell on everybody."

"You wasn't much better," Colette chuckled, finishing her placement of homemade buttermilk biscuits on the sheet before casting them into the oven.

"I was not that bad!"

"Yes you were," Colette countered, "Y'all, that's how she became a journalist. We used to call Sissey, Eye Witness News."

Even Nicole had to laugh, and she bent her head in mock shame.

"I heard about the time you dimed on Bey," Nancy giggled, making a face at Nicole and sticking her tongue out at her, as she moved a filled pan of tomatoes over to the stove to begin frying them.

"Aw, sookie sookie, now. But, you're gonna have to be more specific, Nance—'cause Sissey was always tellin' on Bey." Colette put both hands on her hips and sauntered over to Nicole, who had covered her head in anticipation of a tickle as her sister then began to try to pinch her. "Got Brother incriminated as well. Poor Girard."

"The *Playboy* incident," Nancy said with a wink. "I heard that was one that almost made Mom Johnson lose her religion."

"What?" Deidre exclaimed, looking from one woman to the next while they all slapped each other five and screamed and laughed.

"Y'all telling lies in Mom's kitchen ain't Christian," a male voice boomed from the other room.

"Mind your bizness," Colette yelled back, "if y'all wanna eat sometime tonight."

"C'mon, yall, tell me," Deidre insisted in a conspiratorial whisper. "What'd Bey do?"

"Well," Colette began with dramatic emphasis. "Our poor cousin, Bey, was feelin' Spring mighty hard, you might say."

Nancy shook her head and laughed, bending over the butcher block.

"Had this little church girl in his mind, and she had his nose wide open. Back in the day, Bey couldn't get none, even though he thought he was the lover, with his skinny yellow self. But, Brother—Girard, being older, had gotten ahold of some *Playboy* magazines. Big-mouthed Sissey, our one and only Nicole, told Bey that Girard had a bunch of nasty pictures."

"Uh, ahhh, I did not tell Bey about the magazine, like that. He found it himself! Sort of…." Nicole protested, trying to defend her honor.

"That's not the way I heard it," Colette countered.

"Wait," Nancy added in, pointing her finger at Colette, "Girard never told me it was his magazine…or, that there was more than one. He blamed the whole thing on Bey."

"Why am I not surprised?" Deidre chimed in.

"Gurl, lemme tell ya," Colette giggled, "Girard was fine, I mean tall, dark, handsome, and an athlete. He loved the ladies, and the ladies loved him—and he'd get so close to a kill, then either the girl would get scared, or Nana would bust him before he could go all the way. My poor brother would come upstairs all mean and crabby, hollering at me and Sissey. Then, I would say, betchu didn't get none, did ya? And he'd chase me and pluck me in my head until I cried…or, till I said, I'ma tell Nana."

"How you know all this?" Deidre asked wide-eyed, and hanging on every word.

"'Cause Girard would pay me to keep my mouth shut, and to be his alibi."

"Let the child tell the story," Nancy insisted, becoming engrossed and laughing all the while.

"Like I said," Colette continued, "Girard was always able to talk his way out of a jam. Probably how he ended up as a lawyer. But Nana didn't play no hanky-panky in her house. So, when Girard and us would come down here for the summer, all Girard could do was smooth-talk Mr. Gibson into letting him buy a magazine on the sly. He'd always beg me for my hush money to get it, and I'd say okay—only if he showed me what he bought, and if he gave me fifty cents interest on the dollar. Nobody was gettin' any tail in those days. So the boy was desperate, and I stayed paid all summer…and Girard stayed in the barn, up in the loft, with his secret magazine stash— until Sissey told on him and Bey."

"That's not how it went," Nicole jumped in. "See, Bey took my babysitting money, and tried to go buy a magazine, but Mr. Gibson wouldn't sell it to him…told him to go borrow one of his cousin's. Old man Gibson's daughter overheard it, 'cause she worked at the store in the summers, and she was my best friend, so she told me. So, I told Colette that the same amount of money I was missing was the price of

one of those nasty books. Colette put it together, and
we went up into Girard's hayloft stash, and saw there
wasn't no new issue up there. So I confronted Bey, and
told him that I knew there wasn't no new magazine in
Girard's stash, so he'd better give me back my money.
Then, Bey tricked me, and told me to show him that
there wasn't no new magazine—for evidence, and if
there wasn't, he'd give me the money he supposedly
found."

By this time, every woman in the kitchen was
doubled over with laughter. Female hands waved in
the air, and whimpers and hoots implored the central
storytellers to stop. Poor Deidre squeezed her legs
together tightly and begged the team of Colette and
Nicole to wait for her to recover, lest she pee her
pants.

"Oh, no, we can't stop now. Y'all wanted to
know," Colette panted through the giggles. "Nicole's
got it right. My bad."

Sandra was laid out across the butcher block.
"Stop, please, I can't take it. I can only imagine Bey's
face when he hit the mother-load of Girard's collec-
tion."

"See, Girard is such a liar," Nancy screeched,
wiping her eyes, "He said there was only one magazine."

"One?" Colette nearly yelled.

"Gurl, pulleeease," Nicole went on. "Bey almost
wept when he saw all them big tittied women in
stacks up in that loft. The boy pulled out a knot of

ones, shoved them into my hands, and told me to git. I ran so fast with my loot, that I bumped into Nana on the way to find Colette, and all those bills fell on the floor."

"Oh, my God!" Deidre hollered.

"Nana hauled me into the kitchen, and threatened to take my life if I've been stealing. So I told her that I didn't steal, Bey gave it to me. She asked me where Bey was, and I said in the barn cleaning up. Now, since Bey's narrow, yellow ass wouldn't hit a lick at a snake of chores, Nana knew something was fishy. I wasn't as fast at tellin' tales as Colette," Nicole said with a wink, "so Nana took off with a broom in hand towards the barn, talking about no child of hers was gonna do drugs on her property, 'cause that's the only place Bey coulda got ten dollars—was from selling that whacky weed mess."

"No, lie," Colette reinforced with a hoot. "Nana tore outta this house like a rampaging bull. Poor Bey was up in the loft, surrounded by paper women, his pants down to his knees—"

"Girl, stop it!" Nancy shrieked.

"He started givin' up the tapes as Nana climbed the ladder. The boy was talkin' fast, pullin' up his pants, tellin' her that he found Girard's books and they wasn't his, and Ester was praying out loud to Jesus, calling for Girard, and yellin' to me and Colette to fetch Grandpop and a switch—all at the same time. Nana was talkin' 'bout necket white women desecratin' the sanctity of her home…in between

screamin', 'Jesus, Father, help me,' then she'd go back
to a burst of, I'll kill you dead, boy! Bringing necket-
ness into my house!' Poor Girard was on his way
home with a girl, headed for the barn, when Bey flew
out, Nana on his tail, and me and Colette was runnin'
as fast as our legs could carry us—trying to wave him
down and tell him to go the other way. But honey-
chile, honey-chile—Nana was steam-rolling in his
direction, speaking in tongues, and then, like in slow
motion, Girard turned to run, bumped into his date,
knocked the poor girl down, was trying to get up and
pull her up…. But it was too late. Nana was on him—
beatin' his natural ass in the front yard with a broom,
in front of his date, while she had Bey by the shirt-
tail…callin' them dogs. Grandpop couldn't get to the
boys fast enough. He had to literally pick Nana up by
her waist and carry her into the house. That's the
story, and the only reason Girard and Bey lived.
Grandpop saved them!"

Deidre hauled herself out of the chair and waddled
quickly to the door, tears from laughter streaming
down her face. "Wilton, help me get to the bathroom!
Fast!"

Nicole was standing in the middle of the room
now, stomping her feet, and Colette was leaning
against the sink. Sandra had completely covered her
face with her hands, and a collective scream brought
the men running into the kitchen.

Franklin was the first to burst through the door.
"Everybody all right?" His gaze searched the laughing

faces of the women, and Bey and Girard tumbled in behind him.

Female hands waved and shooed them back.

"Go 'head on," Sandra gasped. "You all don't even need to be in here."

Franklin, Bey, and Girard looked at each other and folded their arms over their chests.

"I think our reputations are under attack, Counselor," Bey said with a chuckle.

"That could be liable. Slander," Girard retorted, then went over to hug his giggling wife. "What lies did you tell them about me?"

"I didn't say a word," Nancy gasped, still unable to recover. "Your sisters told it all."

"Well, since y'all are in here tellin' lies on us," Franklin chuckled, "can anybody tell us when we're gonna eat?"

The pitiful looks on the three male faces at the door brought another round of screams and giggles from the group of kitchen conferencers. But it was Franklin's pained expression of acute hunger that made Colette cross the room to kiss him.

"I haven't thought about or laughed about that mess for years," Colette giggled, still unable to fully catch her breath. "Dinner's in twenty minutes."

CHAPTER FIVE

Laughter rang throughout the house during dinner, until the call for dessert made everyone stand up to make room in their stomachs in order to merely breathe. The entire female part of the family contingent had deftly moved in unison from the dining room into the kitchen, continuing the reverie while they handed dessert plates through the door to men, then received them back—returned with only crumbs. During the process, they had not broken their rhythm while cheerfully cleaning up dinner dishes and putting away the remaining food. The men had brought in a few plates, promising that they would help, but then, one by one, defected into the living room with pie slices to go. By the time the kitchen lights had been turned out, each man had staked out a corner of the room with a drink in hand.

Girard had claimed one of the armchairs by the fire, which in turn meant, the other one, adjacent to it, was for Nancy. Wilton had made a comfortable space for himself and Deidre in the center of the sofa, which also meant that no one else, but Nicole, could fit on it. Bey had pulled two dining room chairs together for himself and Sandra, and Franklin had sprawled mid-floor in front of the fire on the rug.

Colette smiled as she looked at the lounging males. Tradition in this house had not been interrupted, not even by the final passing of Nana, and she wondered how many dinners, holidays, and family gatherings had borne witness to the same, oddly comforting routine?

Her brother was still handsome and athletic looking, with the firelight casting shimmers of gold against the silver gray at his temples and bringing out the reds in his rich, dark chocolate skin. He looked positively regal, and was clearly in charge, as he sat in the high-back chair nursing his brandy. Bey, on the other hand, looked like a graying teenager, and the flickering light brought out the bronze in his complexion that was always cheery, but becoming a little gaunt, she'd noticed. Wilton looked like he hadn't aged a day…still brown, and pudgy with a tender, baby-face. But somehow, her Franklin looked like a lean, sated panther, sensually laid out in the evening light after a healthy kill. He seemed so content that she was almost waiting for him to lick his paws and purr. It was the first time anything in her close to recognizable as being a sexual urge had stirred toward him in a long while.

"Whew, man! You ladies sure out-did yourselves tonight," Girard exclaimed as he rubbed his belly and took a sip of brandy. "Thanks, Bey, too, for providing adequate libations to top off the evening."

"Here, here," Franklin added, raising his glass of cognac in Bey's direction from his outstretched position. "Brother Bey brought a little somethin' to take the chill off after dinner. We thank you, good brother. Ladies, my highest compliments to the chefs."

Bey beamed and nodded. "For real, you all done Mom Johnson proud, and I couldn't come down here without taking care of my boys. And I brought you ladies your favorite wines, too. Our turn to serve you."

"Oh no, not that easy," Nicole laughed. "Breakfast is on you, gentlemen. We left plenty of eggs, bacon, and left-over biscuits in there. I'll take my coffee black and strong, just like I like my men. Thank you."

"No problem," Wilton answered through a sip of his beer.

"Aw, man, don't be givin' in so easy," Bey fussed as he stood and went into the dining room, bringing back stem glasses and an assortment of Merlot, Chardonnay, champagne, and a cold bottle of sparkling cider for Deidre.

"Too late now," Nancy announced, "We have witnesses, and Wilton agreed to it for you, boys. We, the ladies, are sleeping in."

"My wife, the court stenographer," Girard sighed, taking a healthy sip from his goblet.

"That's cool, brothers," Franklin said cheerfully, obviously trying to diffuse a possible gender battle. "Breakfast is the easiest meal of the day."

"Bey...you sweetheart," Deidre crooned, accepting the sparkling cider.

"Yeah, man, thanks," Wilton chuckled, "she's had her eye on my beer all night."

Deidre slapped Wilton's arm and snuggled into him, while Bey poured champagne for Sandra, Merlot for Nancy and Nicole, and knelt to pour a glass of Chardonnay for Colette, then returned to his chair and snuggled up against his date.

The warmth of the fire enveloped the group, interweaving itself between the easy tempo of conversation and soft jazz that Franklin had provided. Colette found herself lying on the floor cuddled into the crook of Franklin's shoulder, the wine taking effect and making her yawn and giggle at the fragments of passing sentences. But every now and then she noticed her sister's far-away look, and how a hint of sadness flickered within her hazel eyes. Her sister's line of vision kept traveling past the group to the photos on the mantle, and Colette said a quiet prayer that one day her sister would have a permanent somebody to lean against by the fire.

"Been a long day of on the road," Girard said in a sensible tone that began dispelling the mood. "We've got a lot of packing and decisions to make in the morning, and maybe it's best that we all make it an early night."

"I hear you, my brother," Wilton yawned, helping Deidre up. "Thanks for putting us close to the bathroom. C'mon, baby, let's get you upstairs to bed."

Nicole stood with them and walked over to the mantle. Her fingers lovingly touched the edges of the picture frames as she considered the photos. "We had some good times in this house," she whispered.

Colette felt a lump beginning to form in her throat. "Tomorrow, baby. We'll figure it all out tomorrow."

Girard nodded, stood, and pushed the remaining embers back deep within the fireplace so that the smoldering timber could burn out on its own. Once he had completed the task to his liking, he held out his hand to Nancy. Being the champion of grace, she made her rounds, kissing everyone good night, then floated out of the room ahead of the rest. The momentary gesture of refinement made Colette smile. Nancy had her ways, but admittedly, she was the perfect match for Girard.

"Well, y'all gonna lie there on the floor all night, or what?" Bey chuckled, helping Franklin to his feet.

"You putting me and Cole out?" Franklin asked with a sly wink before he reached back to pull Colette up.

"Well, now, you gettin' into my bizness," Bey slurred while threading his arm around Sandra's waist, and trying without success to kiss her neck. When she squirmed away from him, he laughed and tried to pull her closer, then gave chase as she fled up the steps laughing.

Franklin chuckled and pecked Colette on the mouth with a kiss before she could say anything, then gave her a wink as he led her out of the room toward the stairs behind Bey. Turning off the lights as they passed each room, Franklin stopped at the base of the staircase and held Colette close.

"Don't begrudge him a little fun for the last time here," Franklin whispered close to her face.

His breath was filled with the sweetness of pie and a hint of cognac, and the warmth of his gentle hug magnetically forced her body to seal the small gap between them. Darkness covered the two as they stood at the bottom of the steps, with only the low red glow from the fireplace making shadows dance against the wall. His kiss began as a soft brush against her lips, then deepened until she could taste the remnants of dessert laced with drink. Yet, it was not forceful. Then, he pulled away, landing tiny kisses upon her eyelids, then down the bridge of her nose, finding her mouth again, and abandoning it for her neck, and the edge of her sweater-covered shoulder.

"This is the best time I can remember in this house," she whispered. "The first time that we all just got along, and nothing came up between any of us."

"I heard you girls laughing in the kitchen, and me and the fellas had a blast trying to figure out which one of us was in the dog house."

"Hmmm…" she murmured through a giggle, as his hands found the center of her lower back. "I'll never tell."

"You sure?" he whispered against her cheek, then grazed her earlobe with a nip.

"I'm sure," she whispered low within her throat, "that you're starting something we can't finish in this house tonight."

He let his breath out slow and warm against her ear.

"I promise to be really, really quiet," he murmured against her neck, "and, to go so slow that neither one of us will care where we are."

The comment combined with the moist heat from his mouth was sending shivers of anticipation through her.

"I'm not making any promises," she whispered, moving away to lead him up the steps, "at least not while everybody is still awake."

She saw him smile from the corner of her eye, and gave him her back to consider as she walked up the steps slowly—very slowly. When she felt his palm graze her backside, lingering for a moment before taking hold of the banister, she swallowed hard. It was going to be difficult to remain respectful in Nana's house, for sure.

"Don't turn on the light," he urged when they entered the room. Gathering her in his arms, he held her in the dark until their eyes focused. "See, isn't this better…and, isn't this why you wanted to be in here? Look out the window."

Moonlight cast a bluish light in the room, and the stars added magnificent splendor. Her body melted against his, and again his mouth captured hers, although, this time, not as tentatively. His hands slipped under her bulky knit sweater and tee-shirt, then began to unhook her bra. As his hands glided around her torso in an upward motion, her skin ignited, setting off a molten flow of desire between her legs.

But a loud creak, then a woman's laughter, made her flinch and giggle, momentarily breaking her trance.

"Oh, Lord. We can't do this. Not with Bey and Sandra at it in the next room."

Franklin chuckled, and released her. "Well let's get in bed. We can't stand in the middle of the floor all night," he quipped in an amiable tone, and stripped before her and tossed his clothes on the floor by the daybed. "Come on, get in, and go to sleep."

"Didn't you bring any pajamas…or, some sweats?" she countered, totally shocked, as she tore off her clothes and found her nightgown in the dark.

"Yeah…I did, but…"

"But, nothing, boy," she laughed in a whisper, "at least put on some pants."

"Yeah, okay," he mumbled, fishing for a pair of sweat pants in his duffel bag at the bedside without getting up. Finding them, he pulled the sweats under the covers to her satisfaction, and motioned for her to join him.

His hot length of skin sent another wave of desire through her, and she chuckled and nipped his chest to chastise him for not having put on the pants he'd found.

"You are really making this hard, for me," she fussed, pushing him away.

"No, correction," he whispered, strategically placing her hand against him, "you are really making this hard for me."

Another deep moan and a loud female gasp from the room next door, followed by the unmistakable rhythmic squeak of springs, made them put their foreheads together and laugh under the covers.

"Oh, my God," Colette whispered, "I can't listen to this."

"From the sound of things, it won't be long now," Franklin chuckled. "I give the brother ten more strokes."

"Shut up, boy…you're terrible!"

Laughter consumed them both, as they burrowed deeper under the covers.

"How're we gonna look Bey and Sandra in the face in the morning?"

Franklin rolled over on his back and pulled the covers down. "After a cold shower and a cup of coffee, I'll be as mean as a hound dog, and it won't matter."

Her laughter joined his as he began counting down and she pinched at his side.

"Ten, nine, eight," he counted, while pushing her hand away, "it's like jazz, all in the syncopation…five…"

"Boy, shut up, before they hear you!" she whispered through her teeth.

"No they won't," he argued, sitting up, "I could be a marching band, and Bey won't know it until......wait a minute, wait a minute...one...done, baby. How much you wanna bet."

"Oh, God, Franklin...there are no words." Colette covered her face with her hands and laughed hard.

"None whatsoever. That's what I've been trying to tell you," he growled, slipping down beside her. "Now, it's our turn."

"Can't we just talk tonight?" she groaned, giving into the hug, but chasing his fingers away from her breast.

"Okay, how about a compromise. You talk, I'll listen, and try to convince you with my mouth not to talk."

"That's not playing fair."

"Uhmmm hmmm," he whispered, trailing from her shoulder down under the covers.

"Just think," she said in a shaky voice, "if it could be like this all the time...if we didn't have to sell this piece of history away, and all of us could come here for the holidays...just like it used to be. Tonight was wonderful."

Her comment made him stop his progressive journey towards her breast, and he brought his mouth up to briefly meet hers. For the first time tonight, and since he'd unloaded his burden on Solomon Whitfield earlier in the day, he remembered his failings.

"Yeah, tonight was the way it was supposed to be," he whispered, then reached down and put on his sweat-pants.

"What's the matter?"

"Nothing," he said gently, coaxing her head back against his chest as he reclined. "You were right…this ain't the place."

CHAPTER SIX

The house was so still in the early morning hours. The sense of peace that engulfed him was both a comfort and a plaguing reminder of what had not happened with Colette. Silence gave him time to calibrate his sense of internal balance, but it also gave him time to think. Too much time, in fact.

He loved his wife. That had never been the question. But, how long would it be before she became disillusioned and dissatisfied with his inability to provide for her in the manner that they'd both always dreamed? His business allowing her to raise a family and work in the community…And, worse yet, what if a baby was never created between them…a child, children, to share in a loving home? In truth, he knew that was all she ever wanted. Not money, not elaborate things…but, a family. That was what he loved so dearly about her. The thought he couldn't reconcile was, how long would it be before her disappointment turned into disgust, and she no longer loved him?

Franklin made his way down to the kitchen in the dim morning light, bent on at least keeping the promise to corral the guys to fix a hearty breakfast. He knew that today was actually D-Day, when all laughter would turn to serious business, and he'd have to quietly witness Colette's childhood being dismantled. In his mind, a good meal together might begin the conversation on a brighter note, giving her another pleasant memory in this house before it became somebody else's.

Entering what had been Mom Johnson's sanctuary, he stood at the threshold and stared out toward the well-equipped terrain. Although he was no stranger to flipping pancakes and scrambling a few eggs for a bunch of hungry mouths—his siblings had been excellent boot-camp preparation for that—it was still somewhat intimidating to try his hand at it in this space. After all, this was the nerve center of the Johnson family home.

A large Mason jar on the counter caught his eye, and he moved toward it with pleased expectation. Colette had remembered. Maybe his fears of her beginning to not care about him the way she'd used to had been just that, a fear, not a reality? As he scooped up the wide-mouthed glass container and inspected it, he was right. Sure enough, his baby had set out some of Mom Johnson's peach preserves. It amazed him how such a little thing could bring so much comfort to his embattled spirit.

The thought of that warm, sweet confection poured over buttermilk biscuits inspired him to hunt in the refrigerator for the eggs, and in the freezer for the possibility of sausage. Then a bright idea flashed into his mind. Fish. Fried, country fish, with bacon, eggs, sausage, and fried smokehouse ham slices. It would be perfect for a peace-summit at the dining room table. He was now on a mission.

To his delight, the freezer in the shed-kitchen offered a selection of frozen meats, and there, in Ziploc baggies, cleaned and scaled, were several local river caught catfish carcasses that had been preserved for a coming meal. He greedily snatched out two heavy-laden bags, and lifted a ham down from the shed hook, before dashing with his loot toward the sink. Now, the question was, how would he defrost the rock-solid quarry? Mom Johnson didn't own a microwave, as the appliance had seemed to go against her religion.

"Well, guess this will have to be done the old-fashioned way," Franklin mumbled to himself as he worked. Pulling out a bowl, he filled it with hot water, and dropped the bags of fish into it.

"Thought I heard somebody moving around down here," Girard yawned, peering at him through sleepy eyes from the doorway.

"Yeah, man," Franklin returned with a smile, "You know if we don't pull our act together this morning, we'll never hear the end of it."

Girard just nodded, and went over to the coffee maker. "I can't get the mental gears rolling until I've had at least the first cup. How long you been up, anyway?"

Franklin glimpsed at Colette's brother from the corner of his eye as he worked on slicing down the ham. "'Bout an hour."

Girard took his time measuring scoops of dark coffee grounds, and adding water, but somehow, both men knew that Franklin's comment wasn't lost in the mundane chore.

"She's taking this hard, isn't she?" Girard finally murmured, as the smell of coffee began to permeate the kitchen and seemed to wake him up.

"Yup." Franklin's response, though terse, was not intended to offend. There just wasn't a whole lot more than that to be said on the subject.

"You all okay?"

"Can't complain." Again, Franklin knew that the short question was loaded, and he felt like a game of Russian roulette had begun.

"I know my sister."

Franklin declined comment and moved over to the drain-board to begin breaking eggs in a large metal bowl.

"I also know," Girard continued, after an assessment of Franklin's non-response, "that she loves you, man. Never forget that."

Although Franklin never turned around, he appreciated the statement. "I love her too…more than I can tell her sometimes."

Girard sat down heavily on a stool and brought his mug of coffee to his lips. He took a deep slurp, closed his eyes, and sucked in the aroma that wafted in the steam above it through his nose.

"Then, why you up so early, and all by yourself?" Girard murmured through another sip, this time bringing the cup away from his face and setting it down on the counter.

For a moment, the two men made eye contact, and Franklin looked away in the direction of the kitchen window without responding.

"That's the kind of situation that you all haven't been married long enough to be going through," Girard said in a low, confidential tone. "That's for me and Nancy, not you."

Franklin stared at the man.

"Look," Girard said hastily, his line of vision traveling out of the door before he leaned in toward Franklin across the butcher block, "I know having to cope with Deidre being here is probably causing a lot of unspoken drama between you—but, you've got time." Girard sat back and picked up his mug again, this time focusing on the dark liquid before he sipped it. "I used to tell myself that it didn't matter…and used to tell her that she was my baby…and, I made it my business to spoil her at every turn…just like Wilton waits on his wife now, hand and foot. But, it never fails. Every time one of Nancy's girlfriends got pregnant, and had a baby shower, or their kid got a first tooth, my poor wife would go into this deep funk. And, no matter what I said, what I bought her, or how I tried to make up the difference, it never made a difference. Got so that time just wore on us, and now, we live in the same house, but we go our separate ways."

Not knowing how to respond to the confession, Franklin watched the pain etch its way across Girard's normally confident eyes. The hurt that emanated back from them tore at his gizzards. At a loss, and wanting to stop his brother-in-law's suffering, he reached for solutions, none of which felt good as they came to his lips.

"Did you ever think about adopting?" Franklin proposed quietly, and not addressing the part of Girard's statement about going separate ways.

Girard's breath pushed out in a heavy, troubled gush. "She wouldn't hear of it, initially. She wanted to be pregnant herself, to experience a life we created together inside of her. Then, all these legal custody battles started coming into the public eye…and time had begun to harden her outlook on such compromises. Franklin, twenty years ago when we married, they didn't have all these fertility treatments, and new technology. In the last ten years, alone, the industry has taken enormous strides, but, alas, my Nancy is beyond the window of time. Her clock ran out. She'll be fifty in March—and she never forgave me…then, she stopped sleeping with me and wrapped herself up in good deeds done through women's organizations and the sorority. And, I became very discrete."

"Damn," Franklin whispered, not knowing whether or not to walk around the counter and give his brother-in-law a hug, or to head for the hills.

"Yeah," Girard whispered back, "you know how hard it is to love your wife more than anything in the world, but to always feel a wall between you? Or, to watch our good brother, Wilton, pull his wife up to him and rub her belly and kiss it, watching his child move within her...or, to hear your boy, Bey, rocking his girlfriend and her calling his name back, the way your own wife used to? That's why I'm up this morning. I thought I would come into this kitchen and ask Mom what to do."

Franklin looked down at the counter as the last part of what Girard had said trailed off with a raspy tone. Dear God in Heaven, no man should have to suffer like that. Every envious thought he'd ever had about Girard went by the by, and he rounded the counter between them to place a hand on his shoulder.

"Yeah, I do know how it feels, man. You ain't alone, but we're all family and gotta help each other through this kinda stuff."

"When I saw you up...I figured something was wrong with you and Colette. I was up all night, couldn't sleep. From the way you two were acting towards each other last night, before we all went upstairs, your room shouldn't have been that quiet. That's how I knew. Once you've lived it, you know it when you see it."

"You know, counselor," Franklin said in an empathetic and paced manner, avoiding the reference to his problems with Colette, "it may be too late to have the children, but, it might not be too late to bring back the love between you?"

"Hopeful thought." Girard iterated in a monotone voice. "I was going to take Nancy down to the Islands for Christmas, since she can't bear to really deal with that holiday—it's really for kids—and all the hoopla around children…thought I'd get her to relax with me down on the beach. That's why I wanted to dispense with this house, and close this door, too, as quickly as possible. No fuss, no muss."

"Then, that's what you should do, man." Franklin tried his best to sound upbeat, but it was obviously having no effect on Girard.

"It's not that simple, although, it could be. Me and Nancy have all the furniture and things we need, and money is not a problem. Bey don't want nothin' but cash—as he's a glass and chrome kinda guy," Girard said with a sad chuckle. "Wilton and Deidre might want a few sentimental items, but, by and large, with a baby on the way, they need to begin a trust fund. Her parents already set them up well, in a very nicely established house on campus when they arranged for Wilton's appointment to the administration. Heavy furniture would just clutter their environment and would not be appreciated."

Girard ticked off his mental laundry list, and Franklin remained quiet, fully understanding that the man had been wrestling with how to dispense of things for a long time. Suddenly, the burden of the responsibility of it all seemed to momentarily eclipse his own problems with Colette. Solomon Whitfield's comments came back to him. Odd, Franklin mused to himself, as Girard droned on, nothing had been as it had originally seemed to be on the surface. What he had, and didn't have, materially, was quickly becoming irrelevant.

"Nicole…well…" Girard went on, "I thought the photos would help her deal, and being single, she could probably use the cash to help her rainy day fund. She's a minimalist and Swedish-modern type, and always traveling, so, what's she going to do with a big floral sofa, huh? Then, I thought about you guys…an infusion could probably help your business, and maybe some of the more substantial pieces of furniture would help give Colette some peace about this. That's why I was pressing for the sale. It would make everybody happy, give us a knot to evenly divide without argument, and, nobody is prepared to live here, pay the taxes and upkeep on it from afar—plus, the likelihood of family gatherings here, after another year or so, will render the point moot. So, I said to myself, Girard, ole boy, you've gotta sell it. I don't know…"

"It's cool, brother. Whatever you decide, it's cool. Nobody's really financially hurting, and—"

"—But, then, I saw Colette and Nicole's faces," Girard protested. "It's not cool. And, it's not going to go as swiftly and cut-and-dried as I'd hoped. My sisters are still not resolved about the sale, and I don't think I can take having them resent me for the rest of our lives. Not for something like this. Not the same way Nancy has kept the frozen undercurrent between us fed…I can't take it from Nance and them too. Can you understand that?"

"They'll get over it," Franklin offered quietly. "Time is all they need."

"No, Frank, you don't understand. Last night, I could see the change-over beginning to happen to Nancy."

"What do you mean?" Franklin held Girard's gaze.

"She was fine, more relaxed than I've seen her in a long time, until she heard Bey and Sandra. Then, the fortress wall went up. She was already on the verge of a bitch-session when Wil was all hugged-up with sweet D. But, the wine, and the good food sort of pre-empted that battle. I even got to kiss her goodnight," he murmured in a far-away tone. "Then, Bey started, and she began cutting up Wilton and Deidre. It was the same old litany about how D was a black American princess without a clue, and how Wil was a weak sonofabitch, who couldn't have achieved anything without his wife's family—so why should they take anything out of the house…yada, yada, yada. Then, she started ragging and going off about how she just wanted to get the hell out of this house. Then she turned on Colette and Nicole, saying they had everything in the world already, and had been spoiled rotten, so why did they need to be worrying about some old stuff that didn't even have real antique value. It was ugly. The only one she didn't have anything to say about was you. I won't tell you what she said about that little girl Bey brought in here. Poor child doesn't stand a chance, now that Nancy has grown fangs again."

"That's deep, brother…I don't know what to tell you."

"Trust me," Girard sighed, then walked over to get a pan for the sliced ham, "when Nancy comes down this morning, she'll be finding fault with everyone and everything."

Franklin shook his head, and let out his breath slowly. "And, that's only going to make Bey snap, and start cussin' and fussin' and drinkin'…and Deidre will be in tears, and Wilton will call his Momma and get her in the middle of it. Man, oh, man."

"And, my sister, Colette, will insist on going through this house with a fine-toothed comb to be sure that nothing of sentimental value is left in it before the realtors come…and, we'll have to get a restraining order on Nicole to keep her from squaring off with Nancy in the dining room."

"And, my wife, your sister, will be done until the end of time. You know Colette. When she's through with you, she's done—and, that's gonna make it real hard for all of us to ever get together under anybody's roof again. We gotta solve this, man. And, you've gotta talk to your wife before she comes down here loaded for bear. I know it'll be hard, and I understand, now, why she is the way she is, but everybody's nerves are on edge. It's going to take time for them to even accept that this stuff in this house has to go up the highway."

"Can I be honest with you," Girard murmured in a low tone, looking up at Franklin like a bewildered child.

The gaze stunned Franklin, and it made him stop all movement.

"I don't know what to do, really. Frank, Nana never had a will. There is no will. She made me the executor, but didn't write anything down. About six months ago, she started talking about missing Grandpop, then called me into her bedroom and had me sit on the side of the bed. Me and Colette knew then that it wouldn't be long.

We never said anything to Nicole. We didn't want her to be afraid, like we were, especially since she was alone. Colette had you. I was the eldest, and a man. That's the way it is."

Franklin's mind tore at the facts and recompiled a million pieces of fragmented conversations with Colette in one instant. His wife knew…she had been afraid…terrified of losing the last parent, and not having given any of them a child as a gift, a remembrance that the line would go on…afraid that there would be no mother, or grandmother, to seek womanly advice from while pregnant…no one to share the secrets of mothering a child in the expert way her own mother and grandmother raised multiple generations…and no grandma days for her child down at the house in Maryland…no summers of fun and pure innocent glee…no repeat of what had made her who she was to pass on to her own. Time had run out, in Colette's mind, and he now understood that, the grieving had really started way back then. If Girard's voice hadn't been so compelling, he would have bound up the stairs and swept Colette in his arms, just to let her know that he'd be there for her, even when the elders could not.

"Man," Franklin whispered, swallowing hard, "you'll do the right thing—by them, and Mom Johnson."

"But, all she'd say was, follow your heart, son. Be fair, and be honest, and keep the family together—and don't let 'em fight like dogs over these scraps of me and your grandfather. I'm countin' on…"

Girard's voice broke, and two large tears filled his eyes and spilled down against his robust, dark face. All authority had gone out of him, and only the man-child remained. Franklin's full embrace seemed to make his shoulders shake, but no sound ever came from Girard as he struggled against the deep well of emotions and gripped onto his dignity in silence.

"The old lady is gone, man," Girard finally whispered, then pulled away from Franklin, rubbed his face hard and stood, his authority having returned instantly. "I'm sorry…it just messes me up, sometimes. They broke the mold...they just broke the freakin' mold. Both Mom, and now, Nana."

"I know, brother," Franklin whispered. "Let's make breakfast."

CHAPTER SEVEN

"You don't need to talk to my lady like that, Nancy," Bey warned as he reached for his second helping from the platter of eggs.

"It's just that, this is family business we're conducting here, and I should think that all non-family members would understand the need to remove themselves from the conversation upon their own volition."

"Thanks for setting out the peaches for me, honey," Franklin interjected, trying to stave off a battle between Bey, Sandra, and Nancy.

"I didn't put out any peaches," Colette quipped, her ire growing as she watched Nancy's pseudo control of the discussion.

Franklin glanced at her nervously. It was in the way his wife snatched up the orange juice container, and set it down just a little too hard before she spoke. He could tell she was near the edge.

"There weren't any peach preserves left, just strawberry. I checked yesterday when I went in the pantry to get the ingredients to make the pies."

Colette's precise diction concerned him.

"And, good pies they were indeed," Girard mumbled through a mouthful of fish, aiding Franklin's attempt to restore civility.

Oh, yeah, Franklin thought, Girard felt it too.

"Well, somebody around here knows peach is my favorite, and I thank you."

The combatants glanced around the room at each other, then dismissed Franklin's comment.

"Well, I would have brought you some up from Virginia, had I known," Deidre added in tentatively, joining the peace-keeping forces. "And, thanks, Colette, for leaving that delicate old christening gown out on the window seat for me and Wilton this morning. It's beautiful. Where did you find it…was it yours, or Nicole's, when you were a baby?"

Confusion captured Colette for a moment, but before she could answer that she didn't leave it, and hadn't seen it, Nancy was on Deidre like a summer wasp.

"First of all, I thought we had all agreed not to start moving things until Girard had gone through the paperwork and final wishes. So, why anyone is leaving things for people, is beyond me."

Colette opened and closed her mouth, stopping her first reaction to curse Nancy out. "I didn't leave the christening gown. I didn't even know Nana had put one up for any of us to use when we had children."

"Well, since that doesn't look like an eventuality for either you or me, Colette, then I guess it doesn't really matter—but, there is the principle of the situation."

Fury tore through Colette, as well as gashed at a very tender, and very secret wound within her. Her gaze narrowed on Nancy. That bitch...

"Gooood morning," Nicole crooned as she slipped into the dining room. "You brothers sure have been burning, and something smells so good!"

Nicole swept past the group, clutching a small photo, and went to wrap her arms around her brother who was seated at the head of the table.

"I love you, Girard," she said with a peck on his cheek, hugging him from behind and closing her eyes. "How did you know this was my favorite picture in the whole house?" She turned the photo over for him to inspect, her eyes glistened with tears of appreciation and joy. "Oh, look at us," she nearly whispered, stooping down beside him. "Nana in the middle on the front steps, you behind her whittling, Colette sitting next to her holding the hair grease—with a fresh done head of plaits, and me in-between Nana's knees, my face all scrunched up, getting mine done. If that doesn't say it all...One day, I'm going to gather up all of these pictures, and do a documentary with interviews of the people who lived in this little town for generations. Oh, Girard...I just love you so much for this."

Bewildered, Girard held the photo in his hands, and looked down at it. "This was on the mantle when we all went upstairs. I didn't leave it."

"Oh, pullease, Girard," Nancy hissed. "You have always spoiled that girl, and it's time to stop. You are going against your own word that nothing in here would be moved, or decided, without group consent. Now, everybody is going for self, collecting stash, and—"

"—What's it to you, Nancy?" Colette fired. "Truth be told, you ain't family!" On that note, she stood, and grabbed her plate and pushed back her chair. "If my brother, Girard, wants to give my sister, Nicole, a picture from our grandmother, it is none of your business. And, if my cousin, Wilton, wants to give his wife, Deidre, a christening gown he found on my grandmother's window seat, it's none of your business. And, if my other cousin, Beynard, wants to share the proceeds of my grandmother's house with his girlfriend, Sandra, it's none of, your, business!"

"It is my business!" Nancy shrieked, standing to follow Colette into the kitchen, "because, my husband, Girard, is the executor of all of your so-called business!"

"No, the hell it isn't!" Nicole screamed behind her, fleeing Girard's side, and following the procession of angry kitchen-bound marchers.

"And, what would you know about the disposition of property, and wills, and legal matters?" Nancy countered, spinning on Nicole, who slid to a halt before her. "You have never been married, never buried anyone without dissolving into a useless heap at the funeral, and definitely have never coordinated anything of magnitude on your own in your life."

"C'mon, y'all, don't fight like this," Deidre begged, searching the faces of the men who seemed to have decided telepathically to steer clear of the fray.

"You're no better," Nancy yelled in Deidre's direction. "Your parents are still here handling everything for you, including your husband!"

"What!" Deidre seethed through her teeth as she wobbled to get up.

"That's enough," Girard warned under his breath in his wife's direction.

"Don't you dare take their side against me—at least not in public!" Nancy's eyes had narrowed to slits as she'd spoken. But, the fact that Girard never lost eye contact with her and had stood up was not lost on the group.

"That's right, you'd better put your woman in check, Brother," Wilton volleyed back in an unsure tone, then seemed to withdraw when both Nancy and Girard turned quickly to glare him down.

"Now, you have gone too far!" Colette yelled as she paced from the kitchen entrance back into the dining room, marching up to Nancy with her sister, Nicole, on her heels. "My brother may not put you in check, but I will. Don't you ever yell at D when she's pregnant, heifer!"

Franklin could tell that Bey and Sandra's smug glances across the table had ignited the situation beyond the point of no return, and had made retreat now impossible for either contestant. Weighing his options, Franklin stood up.

"What did you call me?" Nancy's expression was incredulous, and her voice came out like a low, quiet growl of a guard dog.

"You heard her," Nicole warned in a slow rumble of her own, and angling for the battle that had been long overdue.

Then, there was a moment of silence, just like the seconds before a tornado impact.

"That's enough, y'all. Let it rest," Franklin interceded. "Nobody meant any · harm with the small things that got moved. And, there was no need to call Nancy out of her name, Cole. Everybody chill."

What he was not prepared for was the glare of pure rage that filled Colette's eyes as she stared in his direction. If looks could kill, he would have been laid out cold.

"You're standing here, callin' yourself my husband, and takin' this heifer's side? Are you crazy, Franklin Morris?" Colette's voice was barely audible, but the message was clear. It was on.

"Oh damn…" Sandra and Bey whispered, lowering their eyes and seeming to brace for an unwanted ricochet turn of events.

"Look, Big Sis, Franklin didn't mean no harm," Nicole tried to sooth, coming between Franklin and Colette.

"Get from between me and my husband," Colette whispered through her teeth, "now."

Although Nicole moved away, it was Nancy who stood her ground with haunting satisfaction. She crossed her arms over the chest, creating a slight ripple in her peach silk robe.

"Isn't pleasant to have your husband side with someone else, is it?" Nancy spat out in a venomous tone, "You'll get used to it. Even in public." It was a double-edged, Wilkinson's stainless steel blade that Nancy unsheathed, and it cut down both Colette and her brother in one fell swoop.

"Listen Cole, this is not the place—"

"—No, it isn't," Colette said to him calmly. Too calmly. "Just like it wasn't last night."

When Franklin stepped away from her, she'd been prepared to win the verbal confrontation with him, but nothing could have prepared her for the sheer hurt that etched its way across his face. In the second that followed her lethal interjection, she wished that she could have taken it back. She was hurt, too, and angry, and enraged that he would side with Nancy— but totally unprepared for his reaction to being gored in public. They'd never fought that way—ever. What was worse, was her brother's look of pain as he hung his head and moved away from the table.

It had been a total verbal massacre, and everyone instinctively seemed to know that the battle was over. One by one they each filed out of the room, leaving dishes and food on the table, and heading for a private healing corner of the house. It was time to get dressed and go visit Miss Julia—alone.

CHAPTER EIGHT

Ice crunched beneath Colette's feet as she trudged to Miss Julia's house. Somehow, the brisk pace and stinging cold helped to diffuse her anger. After about a hundred yards, her stride began to slow, just as her patterns of speech had effortlessly transitioned back to her mother-tongue once she felt at home. She took in the serene landscape with newfound reverence. Why Did any of them have to leave from this place?

It was so still and pretty out here, she thought, passing the old Tilman farm and stopping briefly at their gate. Two fat lazy cows roamed in the enclosure and her mind grazed with them, remembering where she'd received her first awkward kiss from Junior Tilman on the front porch after a summer dance. She wondered what had happened to all those kids? Did each child in the town eventually pull away from it to seek their fortunes in the bright lights of the big city? Did they still come home for the holidays, married, with children, returning to the loving arms of parents and grandparents who had held onto this little piece of Heaven for them all?

Colette dragged herself away from the momentary replay of her childhood, and began walking again.

Small crystalline flakes had begun to fall, lightly dusting all that was beneath them, and clinging ever so gently to her lashes. Even with the frozen dirt under her feet, the ground felt softer than city streets.

People had it all wrong, she mused, thinking of how different a snowfall impacted her urban place in the world. True, cities had their conveniences, like buses and trains and easy access to airports and cabs, but there was a softness, if not a tenderness here, that couldn't be denied.

In the city, it seemed, things were physically easier. Flat pavements, street lights to organize crossings, corner stores that stayed open all night, transportation, and a million options of different things to eat, and do. One didn't have to thaw out, or catch, food. You could pick up the telephone and order any type of cuisine, at nearly any hour, from any nationality.

But, here, one had to work at the basics. There were no right-around-the-corner stores. Sometimes, the power went out, and it could be days before the problem was resolved—which meant firewood was essential, and even that had to be chopped and brought in. One had to be physically fit to deal with the long, unpaved stretches between homesteads, she noted as she trudged along. You had to be self-contained on a snowy day, finding ways to amuse yourself in the home with books, and mending, and music. If you had a television, you'd better have cable out here, she chuckled to herself, because the nearest, and poorly stocked, video rental store was in the center of town, along with the gas station, the bed and breakfast, a tiny one-star motel for the en-route-tosomewhere-else-truckers, the diner, the super-market, the bar and pool hall, the hardware store, general store, tobacco shop, and a plethora of little one-product shops, down the street from the school.... and, of course, the church. There was no mall.

However, it was still, oddly, easier. For all of the inconveniences, there were also no sirens, and loud voices, and constant on-guard fears to keep one stiff and mean. People sort of meandered about, and that was okay, because nobody rushed to get to, or to do, anything. The pace, Colette told herself, that was it, the pace was different. Here, the physical amenities required near athletic stamina, but your soul was always at rest. There, in the city, you had every mate-rial and physical want at your disposal, but your soul could die of starvation in the midst of frenetic, joy-less activity.

She stopped briefly to catch her breath as she made it up Miss Julia's path. The frigid weather and long hike had almost stripped the air from her lungs by the time she'd reached her destination but, yet, it felt good.

"My, my, my," Miss Julia exclaimed as she opened the front door, "Now ain't you a sight for sore eyes! Come in here, baby," she laughed, scooping Colette into her wide arms and half smothering her with ample breasts. "Dis here is my Christmas present."

Colette laughed and gave the elderly woman a deep hug before wriggling away so that she could breathe. "I've been so remiss. You're the first person I shoulda come to see…but, there was a lot going on the first day. How've you been?"

Miss Julia sucked her dental plate and flipped her wrist to dismiss the concept.

"Honey chile, you all have plenty to contend with. I knew you'd get to me when the time was right. Now, let's get you some hot tea, and a little somethin' on your stomach, then we can catch up. C'mon into the kitchen. I'm workin' on some pies."

Colette giggled as she followed Miss Julia into the kitchen, knowing that one had to eat as a visitor's rite-of-passage, or major offense would be taken. Down here, food symbolized love, friendship, caring, and could even stand witness as an apology between neighbors. You had to sit down and take your time, and highly compliment all of the superb chefs that labored on the wayfarer's behalf in their alchemy chambers with love.

Entering the small warm room, her eye spotted a basket on the linoleum table filled with a little wiggling thing that gurgled. Anticipation swept through her, and she took off her coat quickly and rushed to the basket, while silently hoping that Miss Julia wasn't in the process of preparing a chicken for dinner.

"A baby!" Colette exclaimed as she moved closer to the basket. "Oh, whose, Miss Julia? Juney had another baby?"

Miss Julia chuckled and came up behind Colette to peer into the basket with her.

"No, this ain't Juney. Dat boy don't need to make no more younguns. Him and Cherl already got six, and about to drive me outta my natchel mind with 'em all running around here."

Colette giggled and leaned into the basket as the baby curled a fat fist around her pinky finger and hung on.

"She likes you," Miss Julia cooed. "Ain't she just a precious angel."

"Oh, yes…" Colette whispered, looking down into the round, wide eyes and chubby little face that greeted her with a smile. "Just look at this child…"

The elderly woman let her breath out slowly, and moved to the stove, then brought Colette a hot biscuit with jam and tea. "Beautiful little thang almost didn't make it here, and didn't half stand a chance," she sighed, turning Colette's attention away from the baby's face for a moment to stare at her.

"Triflin' mother," Miss Julia explained with defeat, going back to her post at the sink. "You know, Juney lives here with me, since Paul passed. Him and Cherl didn't have nowhere to go, and he used to look in on your Grandmaw, and old man Tilman. My other younguns been tryin' to coax dem two to follow behind them to Washington, but, Juney stays here to look out for me and Miss Pat, Cherl's Momma. Her Momma's my other best friend, next to Ester, who's gone now. She got three daughters of her own, all livin' in the city with their kids living with her. Ester woulda took the baby, when Reverend came to us with her. But, then, Ester closed her eyes."

"But, where's the baby's parents?" Colette asked, unable to follow the long weaving trend of the explanation. In reflex while still standing, she bit into the biscuit and sipped the tea—her finger still locked in the baby's grip.

"Drugs. Died on that crack. Don't know how, but the Lord spared the chile any defect. The girl passed right before her Momma. Some say, seeing the daughter die, killed the mother. They don't know who or where the father is…and, I suspec' he ain't worth findin'—so, Reverend brought her to Ester, then to me after Ester passed. If it hadn't been for the fact that Juney looked in on Ester every day, and Solomon Whitfield told that he hadn't seen Ester that morning when he delivered the mail, that po' chile mighta cried herself to death and coulda starved in the house all by her lonesome."

Colette sat down slowly, and could only stare at the elderly woman who was now lacing pie-crust with apples. "But, Miss Julia," she whispered, ignoring her tea and biscuit. "You've got so many children of your own, and they have children…and all of the town is mostly grandmothers and seniors, all of whom have a lot of grandchildren to watch. Didn't the girl have any sisters or brothers who'd take the baby?"

"Not a one left livin'," Miss Julia said with a huff. "The city kilt 'em all, that's why her Momma took to her bed and called upon Jesus to bring her home."

Miss Julia stopped her pie-making and looked at Colette. "You know, me with my arth-a-ri-tis, and Pat, with her bad hip…and, all our chillen barely makin' due…we couldn't put this baby on a generation down. So, me, I said, da Lord don't put no more on ya, den ye kin bear. And, I figured, I'm not long for Glory, myself, so, I best not be turning away no lamb of da flock. You know what I mean?" Before Colette could speak, she went on. "When ole Rev brought this bundle to me, I said, Now Julia Davis, dis here might jus' be your last blessin' from above. You never know what's in a chile of God. Amen. So, I signed them papers to keep her. And, that's all there is to tell about it."

The firm dignity and sureness with which Miss Julia had spoken made Colette sit up straighter in her chair. She searched the lined dark face to understand where the well of strength came from, fully knowing that this was how black people had made it from slavery to freedom. Unconditional love, extended families, people going above and beyond and making a way out of no way. And, with that glimpse into the strength of age and wisdom before her, came her shame. How meaningless had all of her family squabbles been in the face of such adversity, and unwavering faith?

"Let me bring you some things from the house, at least," Colette murmured, not knowing what else to say.

"Chile!" Miss Julia scoffed with a wave of her broad hand. "We don't need a thing."

"But—"

"—But nothin', baby," Miss Julia soothed in her timeless, buttermilk smooth voice. "Your grandmother gave us everything we'll ever need. Like dis here apron, dat I'll cherish till I see her again. And," she said, holding up her hand to stop the protest, "she gave us blankets, and children's clothes for all my grands, not to mention, all her front yard hens. Ester would bring a little gift for each of us at the church every Sunday, that's how we knew she was markin' time. Even gave Juney some tools, so he could keep fixin' people's houses, and work on cars in town. But, most of all, she gave us all of her love while she was here. That's tucked away safe in my heart. She was my best-ever friend. Don't need no mo' den dat."

Colette watched tears well up, and then fade away from the old woman's eyes that shined with unashamed emotion.

"I miss her, too," Colette whispered.

"We all do, baby, but that's jus' how life goes. It was her season, and she lived a good, clean Christian life—so, the Father called her home." Julia Davis crossed the small kitchen and placed a warm thick palm against Colette's cheek. "Now, you lissen here," she whispered. "Ester ain't gone, she right there with you like an angel on your shoulder. I talk to her all da time."

"You do?" Colette murmured, covering the gnarled hand with her own.

"Oh, yes, siree!" Miss Julia chuckled, removing her hand from Colette's cheek to dab the corners of her eyes. "In fact, I fussed hard at Ester the other day when this here chile was ballin'. I said, Ester Johnson, you the one named after the good woman in the Bible, the one who supposed to be watchin' babies past your season. You the one who done raised fine, educated children, with good children of they own— so, you the expert, not me," she laughed again. "So, why I gots to be the one here with this squawlin' little thing? You were the calm one, the smart one. Me, I was the wild one. So, what I'm supposed to do?"

Colette laughed, trying to conjure up the image of a wild Miss Julia in her mind, to no avail. The image was too incongruent.

"Well," Colette chuckled, "you still are a looker, Miss Julia, and have enough energy to get Mr. Tilman to help you out, I'm sure."

Miss Julia laughed harder and placed a kiss on Colette's forehead. "Mayhaps I do, chile," she giggled. "But, these days, the only thing that I can do to warm him up and git his motor runnin', is to bring him a hot pie. Now, a few years ago, mighta been able to intres' him wit someth in' else."

The shock that swept through Colette had obviously registered plainly on her face, because Miss Julia's response to it was to laugh even harder.

"Now, jus' 'cause we seniors don't mean that all the life done gone outta our bones. A man is still a man," she chuckled, moving back toward the stove. "Speakin' of which, how's that Franklin of yours?"

Before Colette could formulate an answer, Miss Julia began again. "Now, that's a man," she pronounced. "A good one. Hard-workin', kind, responsible, good-lookin', too. Ester tol' me all about him. Wish my own dang kids had followed suit. Been tellin' Juney to get over there and talk to your Franklin, while y'all here, so maybe he could learn himself a thing or two 'bout auto-mechanics, and could learn how to open his own real business, instead of piece-mealin' his way through life. Ac'chally, Franklin could teach a lotta dese fellas dats left 'round here how to do. You know?"

Colette just nodded, but didn't speak. Too many thoughts jumped through her mind to sort them out before Miss Julia started up again.

"Now, you look at this here town," the older woman warned. "See, all the young has gone out of it, and the ones dats left, ain't worth a damn, pardon my French, Jesus. All us grandmaws and grandpaws is raising babies they made out in the city then bring home, or providin' room and board for everybody. The men my Juney's age, don't know what to do wit deyselves, and the women dats left, humpf," she added in disgust. "Can't tell which is mother or chile."

"There's a few jobs and stores left, Miss Julia. And, I know Doc Miller still needs help."

"Yeah, I suppose, but ain't nobody to pass on knowhow to. Like, what's gonna happen when old Carter can't fix cars no mo', or Doc Miller finally retires, like he shoulda ten years ago, or Doc Pearson gives up on doin' people's dentures? An', who's gonna take over Gibson's General Store, huh, tell me? It's enough we's raising all the babies, we can't run all the businesses too, and keep house, and everything, honey. Ain't no replacements. Sooner or later, everybody gonna haft to travel for miles to Virginia or Washington to get anythin' done, and at our age, that's more than a notion."

"Maybe…" Colette's voice trailed off. What could she say?

"We's tired," Julia Davis exclaimed with righteous determination. "Broke down, like old Georgia cotton mules. But, we gotta press on, 'cause all dese little chillen don't have nothin' to do, nothin' to expand dey minds, and there ain't much recreation we can provide. Only a few teachers left, and dey don't even teach Negro history good any more. If we don't watch ourselfs, 'fore long, this will be a ghost town, and we'll all be turnin' in our graves watchin' properties get sold, and all the history lost, like what almost happened when Angela Snowden came."

"This town used to be so lively, and has so much potential…that would be a crime," Colette whispered in agreement.

"Uhmmm hmmm," Miss Julia confirmed. "Is hallowed ground, too. Did you know that the Indians had it first, but no tribe claimed it, so they never warred over it. In fact, they say, no blood ever spilt here in no war. It was the pass-thru, fer white, black, and red alike, they believed, from this world to the spirit world. It sat on the border of three tribes, don't remember which, but it was considered the safe haven, and it turned out to be so for colored folk."

"Didn't the church take it over first?" Colette said in a distant voice, trying to scavenge the remote facts in her mind.

"Yep, da white Methodists bought these twelve square miles, and it was abolistionist territory, before AME took it over. They willed each parcel to the colored and Indian families that escaped up here, and anointed every property with oil in a big call-on-Jesus ceremony. Made even the Klan scairt to come on people's land, so, anyone who built here felt protected. Strange, but, no matter what was going on, things would happen all around this town, but never to the town. Was only like fifty original families, Johnsons and Davises among 'em. Colors sorta all blended together, 'cause we was all so close-knit. Den, people had children, who married children. Humph," she exclaimed, "probably everybody here's related, in one way or another…so, how'd I know if this pretty little baby girl wasn't one of mine no-way?"

As she stood, Colette gazed at the caramel face and wide brown eyes again, leaning into the basket to kiss the baby's warm cheek. The wafting scent of fresh, new life filled her nostrils, and her arms ached to scoop up the bundle and press the child to her breasts.

"May I," she whispered, looking toward Miss Julia for permission.

"You sure can," Miss Julia graciously offered, "but, be careful, she'll grow on you."

Reaching down ever so tentatively, Colette slid her hands under the child's body, supporting the wobbly head with her palm. She cradled the infant against her, nuzzled her face against the tender flesh, and breathed in the child's scent with a sigh. "Oh, you are such a beautiful gift to the world, and so lucky to have a Mom-mom Julia to raise you up," she cooed, "God bless you, little one." Tears blurred her vision, and Colette carefully returned the infant in the basket, knowing that a stronger dose of holding her would make it impossible to part with her.

"Look like you a natchel," Miss Julia beamed. "Holdin' a baby like dat, when you jus' married, they say, brings on good luck. I'ma say me a prayer, or two, on it. Just keep da faith, chile."

Somehow, the old woman's words brought a sense of immediate comfort that she could have only received from her own Nana's mouth. Colette knew that what Mrs. Julia Davis had said was not only a blessing, but a promise, that had been given to her in that simple statement. It was a commitment to contact God directly on her behalf, and to pray that a child would come into her and Franklin's lives…a perfect baby, at the right time…and knowing that she'd receive said blessing, she could go back to the house filled with spirit and patience. An elder woman-shaman-survivor had filled her body with food, her mind with history, and her soul with hope, and only an elder from back home could perform such kitchen magic…this was what she'd needed from Nana. Colette considered the sense of community and lineage that went back countless generations. They were indeed all one family, one tribe, and one enduring testimony of survival.

"Well, Miss Julia," she said quietly, "I need to get back and start the process that I came down here for."

"But, you hardly touched your tea, and just took one pitiful bite of that biscuit."

She looked at the old woman's crestfallen face, and crossed the room to hug her.

"I'll be back," Colette promised, "and, I won't be empty-handed. I'll have some of Ester's strawberry preserves for you. There's plenty to share. Franklin ate up the one jar of peaches he found."

"Now, for that, and the company, I'd be much obliged," Miss Julia murmured, squeezing Colette to her harder. "Nobody made preserves as well as our Ester. But, I'm surprised Franklin found peaches," she said with a puzzled look. "We only put up strawberry this year." She dismissed the thought with a smile. "No matter."

"And, my manners are really long gone," Colette added with shame, "I didn't even thank you for filling up the freezer, and cleaning the house so nice. You didn't have to go to the trouble…making all those beds…We really appreciated it, honestly."

Miss Julia laughed, and kissed her. But her expression contained a hint of curiosity.

"Baby, now you know, I can't take the credit for all-a that. Me and Pat sent Juney to go fetch the laundry, and we had him carry everything back to the house. We told him to deliver my note when he did— put it on the fridge to letcha know the laundry was done. He just put away the linens in the closet like we asked him to, knowing y'all was comin,' and had him put a few little odds and ends in the ice box for ya, that we pulled together—but, we didn't go to no lengths. Was anything missing? Why, I'll tan that boy's—"

"—Oh, no!" Colette assured her, becoming alarmed that such a concept would ever enter Miss Julia's mind. "I guess we have Juney to thank, then, for not only salting the driveway, but for cleaning up the entire house. I just assumed it was you?"

"Do, say…" Miss Julia began slowly, her gaze becoming distant. "Now, my Juney wouldn't clean no house, not even for a million dollars. And, as to my cleanin,' and such—there was a day when it wouldn'ta been a passin' thought to do for a neighbor…Then came my Arthur, which don't allow me to bend and git 'round like I used to, and dear Pat, her hip is so bad, she kin barely make it up da steps. But, lest I forget, lemme give you back the key. Like I said, as to food, we put a few eggs and stuff in there, like I said in that little note—all so's you'd know what was in there. We didn't have to add no meats or can nothin', 'cause you know your grandmother, she had everything put up and ready for the holidays—just like she always did, God bless her soul. You know how she'd put up November greens and freeze 'em… No baby, since Ester was doin' good on her feet, we just didn't think that far."

The two women stared at each other without breaking their embrace.

"The house was spotless," Colette whispered.

"Well," Miss Julia shrugged. "Is it any wonder? That was our Ester."

CHAPTER NINE

As she made her way up the path towards Nana Johnson's house, Colette paused for a moment. Something was wrong. Where was Girard's black Mercedes, and Beynard's red BMW?

She quickly bounded up the steps, inserted the key in the door, and breezed into the house. Wilton greeted her with an expression on his face that told her not to speak until they could get close enough to one another to whisper. From his reclining position on the sofa, he reinforced the telepathic message by looking up from his laptop computer, briefly casting his line of vision toward the kitchen, and putting his finger to his lips to ensure her silence.

"What happened?" she murmured, as he made room for her to sit next to him. "Where is everybody?"

"Brother is in the kitchen, cleaning up from breakfast. Franklin's out back—and has been out there, chopping wood, for the last hour and a half. Bey, Sandra, and Nicole took Bey's car and went into town to the diner, since everybody refused to eat another meal together. Deidre is finally taking a nap, and I'm going to take her into town to eat when she wakes up soon."

"And, Nancy?" Colette whispered hard. "Where's she?"

"Oh, gurl," Wilton said with a deep rush of air, "She left him."

"What?" Incredulous, Colette leaned into Wilton and held his arm.

"After you went down to Miss Julia's, Colette, all hell broke loose." Wilton glanced toward the kitchen door, and began again, only when he was convinced that he could speak confidentially. "It's so complicated, I'm not even sure I can pull it all together in the right order. But, here's the best to my knowledge. Nancy and Girard went into their room, and stared hollering and screaming at each other."

"Wait," Colette demanded under her breath, trying to gather her thoughts and picture the scenario. "My brother was hollering?"

"You gonna let me tell you what happened, or keep interrupting until Brother comes in here?" Wilton fussed through his teeth.

"Okay, okay, I'm sorry, but, I just can't imagine…"

"Yeah, neither could we," Wilton admitted. "We all know that things get strained between them two, every now and then, but they were really going at it…bringing up things that shouldn't be said…and, talking divorce."

"What!"

"I said," Wilton reminded her, "let me finish." Once he seemed appeased that she wouldn't interject, Wilton continued. "I didn't think it was my place to go in there, unless it got physical." Wilton ignored the shocked expression on Colette's face, knowing that she now understood just how heated the argument had become between her brother and sister-in-law. "But Bey and Sandra ran down the hall."

"Oh, my God…" Colette couldn't contain herself, the comment had come out from sheer reflex as her hand covered her mouth. "Where was Franklin?"

"Outside, I told you. Now be quiet, I've gotta get through this fast." Receiving Colette's nod, he picked up where he'd left off. "I heard Bey, which I knew was going to boil the pot over. That's when D and I went across the hall into the room. We thought they'd be squared off, but instead, we saw Bey sitting on the edge of the bed, wailing…somebody had left Nana's silver heart locket—with a picture of the four of us when we were boys, on his bed…musta been while we were down at breakfast, and they also left Grandpop's gold pocket-watch on the chair in Bey's room. Sandra was on her knees in front of Bey, trying to get him not to cry, and he was blubbering—I'm telling you, baby-wailing, telling Girard how much the tiny locket-photo meant, how good Nana and Pop had been to raise him, since his own mother was so trifling and his own father had left…all how they was the only family he had, and we were his brothers, not his cousins, in his mind. That's when Nancy went off, stormed out of the room and challenged Nicole."

"Oh, damn...."

This time, Wilton kept pace despite her interjection. "That's what I said. Nicole was packing to leave on the next thing smokin' when Nancy burst in her room, and accused her of giving Bey valuables without telling anybody. Nicole—and you know littl' sis—flipped, claiming she didn't give anybody doodley-squat. Nancy called her a bold-faced liar, and that's when Nicole cussed Nancy out so bad that, even me and Girard had to stop it. That's when Nancy started screaming about how he didn't need to protect her from his bitch sister, then slapped Girard's face, and everything went still."

"Oh. My. God." There were no further words that she could employ as she stared at Wilton.

"I thought Girard was going to deck her, and me and Bey jumped up and grabbed his arms outta instinct. I mean, it was the look in his eye...I've never seen Girard's face look like that. Then he left the room, and came down to the kitchen. Nancy grabbed her suitcase and headed for Miss Ruth's bed and breakfast in town. Me, Bey, and Deidre ran behind Girard, but he told us to get away from him, it was over. Nicole went out back to get Franklin to talk to Girard, but he said, it was married folks' business, and this was a long time comin'—and he kept choppin' wood. Baby-doll, this is the worst it's ever gotten in this family."

"And, you're in here doing University work, instead of talking to Girard?" Colette stood up with disgust.

"I'm working on my novel, if you must know," Wilton hedged defensively. "It's the only thing that gives me any peace any more."

She stared at her cousin. "Your novel? Since when—"

"—Since my wife's family took over my life!" he suddenly yelled, breaking the whispered exchange. "Every man has to have something to claim as his own—to be proud of accomplishing on his own. Yes, even quiet, book worm, fat Wilton, okay!"

Again, all she could do was stare at her cousin as he now stood and glared at her. "Wilton," she began quietly, "I never—"

"—Never thought it mattered, huh, Colette? Never thought I had any dreams or aspirations, or even a god-damned backbone! Never thought me and Deidre haven't gone through our problems, or ever thought about what's it's like to have your whole career decided for you, and to not be able to touch your wife for a year because she might lose the baby you've had to go to a fertility specialist to make? I'm going to the diner after I get D up, and we may even stay in the hotel in town. I hate this house, and don't want a thing from it—not the money, not the furniture, and not the memories, nothing. Bey and Nicole said the same thing, as did, ironically enough, Nancy. Funny how things work out," he raged through his teeth, then spun on his heels and stormed up the steps.

She stood in the middle of the living room floor for a moment, trying to process everything that had been said, and had occurred, and every emotion that the series of outbursts had invoked. What was happening to her family? Girard's slamming of pots and pans drew her into the kitchen.

Entering the room quietly, she slipped in and found a perch on one of the tall stools. From her seat, she watched him move around without speaking, fully knowing that he was aware of, but ignoring her presence.

"Rough morning," she murmured, in a feeble attempt to coax him into a conversation.

"So, you've heard," he grumbled back, working without making eye contact.

"You need to go get her," she whispered. "She's hurting bad, I'm sure."

"And I'm not!" he yelled in a sudden outburst. "I'm not?"

"You both are, and have been," she said calmly, keeping her voice even. Standing, she walked over to the wounded bear that was her brother, and risked getting bitten. But, for some reason, she was not afraid. Years of watching Nana heal hurts ebbed into her cellular memory, and she reached for her brother despite his protests, wrapping his rigid form in her arms. "Go to her, Girard, and tell her how much you need her to be in your life."

His body grew stiffer, yet his voice gave way to a gravelly tone when he attempted to argue. That's when she knew for sure, there was hope.

"There's too much water under the bridge, Colette." His voice quavered and he took deep breaths in between each word. "It's not all her fault, either."

"I know," she whispered against his shoulder, "and it's not all yours, either."

Her comment drew his arms around her, and he released deep breaths of attempted emotional control against her hair.

"I wasted so much time, Cole...I started off doing what I loved. I should have kept working on civil rights claims with the NAACP. But, it didn't pay well. Ambition took hold of me, and I told her we should wait until I got a better job. And, she listened to me. Then, high-stakes corporate law got good to me...it possessed me, and the adrenaline rush, and feeling of power when I won a big case. I was moving up, made partner, then senior partner, and she was always there—the perfect executive's wife, assisting my career rise, and every year that went by, I kept saying, not yet, when the time's right...until we ran out of time, and she started hating me. She had a right to, because I cheated her out of creating life itself...I got the things I wanted, but never stopped long enough to realize, all she ever wanted was children. All the material possessions and fat bank accounts were what I needed to make me feel whole. I was so afraid of not making the grade, not living up to her and her family's expectations, and being thought of as some country bumpkin…"

Colette rubbed her brother's back and swayed against him in the timeless rocking rhythm that soothes the soul of even the most savage beast. She closed her eyes and said a mental prayer, and in that moment, she saw her own Franklin's struggle. The image was so clear, so recognizable that, it brought tears to her eyes. "Go to her, Girard. Go bring your wife home for the holidays."

"I can't," he whispered. "She won't have me, and I don't blame her. I can't remember the last time I even touched my wife…got so that I started working late, but she knew what that meant…even though I only go out like that now, maybe once every coupla months…still. There's so much water under the bridge. I can't even admit it to you, let alone myself."

Colette held her brother back and looked at him tenderly. "Do, or did, you love any of them?" she asked in a quiet, but firm tone.

"No," he confessed, then dropped his gaze. "All I want for Christmas is my wife back."

"Then," she murmured, tracing his tears away from his face with her forefinger. "I suggest you go downtown and pick up your present."

—∿—

"Now, Girard Johnson, boy, come on over here and give Miss Ruth a hug!"

Girard leaned across the front counter of the bed and breakfast inn, forced a smile and complied, trying his best to camouflage his distress and nervousness about having to inquire about his wife's whereabouts.

"Oh, my goodness, it's so good to see you," the elderly lady exclaimed, rounding the desk, and bringing him a key. "Now, lookie here," she whispered, "it ain't my bizness, but I'm an old wide woman, and kin see what don' hafta be said. You go on upstairs and tend to ya wife. She came in here all upset and cryin', and I know she love you, 'cause she wouldn'ta been a-weepin' her eyes out, tryin'ta act all reserved, and what not, if she didn't…and, I know Ester Johnson's boy ain't do nuthin' too despicable to no woman. So. There's hope. Mr. Whitfield even brought her your letters. So. I know you wanta reopen a conversation with her, and she don't look like da type to be runnin' on 'er husband. So. Like I said. Dere's hope."

The intimacy of the town wore on his nerves, but in that moment, all he could do was accept the key with grace, kiss the old lady's forehead, and quicken his pace up the steps to find his wife.

Nancy let out her breath in exasperation as she heard the key in the door. The old woman who ran the place had practically talked her ear off with non-requested Biblical marital advice, given that it was slow season—and all Mystic Ridge visitors were staying with family members, and not another guest was around to distract her. She wiped her face with the backs of her hands, and then quickly folded the letters in her lap.

When Girard's form entered the room, a wave of relief washed over her. New tears filled her eyes, and this time she allowed them to drop without censure.

"I read your letters," she whispered to him as he closed the door and faced her.

"I didn't write any letters," he managed, not moving from where he stood.

"Yes, you did," she murmured, standing up, and grasping the envelopes, as well as a small purple ribbon. She extended the evidence in her hands for him to inspect, but stayed close to him. "You wrote your Nana all the time…and told her how much you loved me…and asked her advice…and told her how sorry you were that no grandchildren were on the way."

As she kept her gaze fixed upon him, he reached out and touched the moisture on her cheeks and trailed his fingers in them. "I felt so guilty, baby…I wanted Nana to tell me something, anything at all, that I could fix this…that I could give you something, anything to make up for it…I even prayed to God, but He didn't hear me…and, I asked Nana to help Him hear me…"

She brought her fingers to his lips and stopped the flow of words, then replaced her fingers with her mouth for the first time in many, many years.

CHAPTER TEN

Colette kept stirring the large pot of homemade soup that had absorbed her thoughts as she listened to the sound of the back door banging open. She didn't flinch, or look up from the steaming vessel as a cold blast of air whipped about her.

"Mighty chilly out there," she remarked casually, stirring the rich mixture of ham chunks, lima-beans, and vegetables. "Want a warm up?"

"I'll be just fine," Franklin grunted, hauling an armload of wood through the door into the living room.

The heavy thud of timber hitting the fireplace traveled into the kitchen, and she smiled. "Was that you, or the wood? Even a workhorse's gotta eat, or fall down dead."

"I told you, I'm fine," he bellowed, then paced across the floor and out to the back yard.

"That you are," she yelled behind him in a good-natured tone.

When he came in again, his pace had slowed a bit, but she could tell that he was still very annoyed.

"Two bowls are in the dining room, with some hot tea and biscuits. Care to join me, or, are you going to go to the diner like everybody else did, and leave me here all by myself?"

Although he didn't answer, this time, he closed the back door, kicked the snow off his boots and grabbed a mop. She watched him from the corner of her eye as he cleaned up the chunks of packed snow that had fallen on the floor, returned the mop to the shed kitchen, and took off his coat, cap, and gloves, carefully placing them on the radiator to dry. Still, without a word, he went to the sink, washed his hands, and then went into the dining room. She smiled from the doorway between the rooms as he stood at the table for a moment, looked confused, then relaxed—seeming quietly pleased that she had put a bowl at the head of it where Girard normally sat.

Colette slid into the seat adjacent to him and bowed her head, and said the short meal-time prayer that had been ingrained in her since childhood. When she looked up, he dropped his gaze down to his bowl and began to heartily devour its contents.

"Need to talk to you, Franklin," she said in a slow easy manner.

"Can't a man eat in peace, Colette?" he grumbled through a slurp, then broke off a piece of biscuit and sopped at the thick concoction in his bowl.

"Been owing you an apology," she said plainly, glimpsing him from the corner of her eye.

His grunt was all the affirmation she required, and his moodiness made her smile widen—despite her attempts to hide it.

"You know, sometimes a woman can be wrong," she said casually, and his scoff made her chuckle.

"She can be wrong for a long, long time, did you know that?"

"We can just let sleepin' dogs lie," he mumbled. "It's squashed."

"Naw," she countered, chuckling when he cast a glare in her direction, "a dog that sleeps too long can get up mighty evil in the morning."

"Now, what's that supposed to mean?" he huffed, then washed down his mouthful of biscuit with a swig of tea.

"Means that, a woman can be wrong for like…I don't know, six months, or more, and not even know it."

He stared at her for a moment, then went back to his soup.

"Then, if she's not careful, six months can go to a year, which can go into many years…and, then, the dog either gotta runaway to get fed, or gotta be put outta its misery, once it's gone mad and turned."

"Colette, I'm not getting into your brother's business. Girard's a grown man, and—"

"—And, I'm not talking about Girard and Nancy."

"So, what, then? Me and you?"

"Anybody else in this house?"

"I can't rightly say. Been outside minding my own beeswax."

She laughed, and began eating her soup.

"Yeah, guess a person could, and should, mind their own business, but, in this town, that's hard to do."

He glimpsed up at her, then stood, taking his empty bowl into the kitchen. She could hear him dishing himself another bowl, and she waited for him to come back and sit down before she continued.

"Seems like nothing got moved, or done, but a lotta arguing and fussing this past few days, and its almost Christmas Eve."

"I knew this was how it was gonna go down," he muttered, "and why I said it coulda waited until after the holidays."

"That's one of the reasons I owe you an apology," she said amiably, finishing her own soup in the long stretches between their comments.

After he turned his bowl up to his mouth, polishing off what remained in it, she took his dishes along with hers into the kitchen—not surprised that he followed her.

"You didn't have to dress me down in front of your family, though," he countered in a low voice, with his comment aimed at her turned back.

"No, I didn't," she said quietly, rinsing the bowls and spoons and tea-cups.

"It was a pure lack of respect," he argued on, his voice issuing from low in his throat with hurt.

"It was, and very inconsiderate."

She turned around and looked at him, and his gaze slid to the floor.

"I may not have degrees and money, and all, but I'm still a man, and have my pride, Colette."

He was on the other side of the butcher block, and she knew that closing the space between them was imperative now. Slowly making her way to him, she touched his jaw-line and brushed his mouth with a kiss when she reached him, then pulled back so that she could look him directly in the eyes.

"I'm sorry," she whispered. "For real, for real...and not just for today. But, for the pressure."

Franklin shrugged and then nodded.

"I saw first hand what it can do. I saw it in Girard, in Bey...in Wilton...my Lord."

Again he nodded, but this time his stance relaxed enough to accept an embrace from her.

"Where's everybody?" he whispered, while enfolding her in his arms as he'd asked the question.

"Girard went to go bring his wife home," she murmured against his cheek. "Wilton went to feed his wife and join Bey, Sandra, and Nicole at the diner."

"If it keeps snowing like this, they'll all have to wind up staying in town at Miss Ruth's," he whispered slowly, closing his eyes as her lips caressed his neck.

"Yeah, and they'll all come home here, tomorrow morning, after Juney plows the road...to pick up their clothes, and get on the road," she said in an even lower tone aimed at his ear, and designed to send a warm rush of breath into it.

"Uh, you think so?" he barely whispered back, pulling her against him harder.

"I hope so," she murmured as her mouth found his and captured it.

"Then, let's go upstairs."

—◆—

The long walk through the house, up the steps, and down the hall to their room had been cloaked with silent understanding. Small twinges of anticipation made flip-flops inside her lower belly that gradually singed her inner thighs as her husband held the door open for her—then locked it behind them. No words we're exchanged as he held her gaze and gently unbuttoned her sweater, peeling layers of winter clothing off, and trailing kisses against her flushed skin as each garment was removed. She returned the favor, and was rewarded with his deep gasp each time her mouth found a new section of his skin to adore.

Desire returned, unfamiliar, yet recognizable, and he seemed to revere it with trembling hands that played in the key that also understood that it took time to love a woman…a chord of love sublime that insisted on taking its sweet ole' time to arch her back and make her knuckles turn white as she grasped the corners of the sheets…baby, please…and she seemed to remember the song better now upon each slow, burning thrust…it was the memory-laden instinct of how to follow his lead, and lead him to follow her anywhere—because she fully loved him back enough to make him call her name, and to bring tears to the man's eyes that she cherished, oh, so much…not yet…just as her body remembered how minutes could feel like hours, and hours like minutes, until time stood still, and the metronome in their bodies and breathing synchronized, and repeated the stanza of short breaths that led to deep, resounding moans of syncopated rhythms that oozed into shudders, and off-key sharps and flats which snuck up on you as they slid up and down the scale of a backbone, and ended on a pant then a sigh. Oh yes, she remembered the music that they'd once listened to together…it was called real jazz.

Dawn washed across them, and she turned over lazily to break their fitted-spoons position to find his mouth for a kiss. "Baby," she whispered. "You hungry?"

"Hmmm…" he grumbled low in his throat. "Starved."

"Wanna raid the refrigerator?" she chuckled, snuggling against him.

"Yeah, but my legs feel like Jello," he murmured, then kissed her deeply. "What time is it?"

"C'mon, man," she giggled, reaching over to the nightstand to turn and see the clock. Then she stopped and drew herself up into a ball at the headboard, gathering her knees under her arms and began to rock.

Franklin immediately sat up and reached out for her, looking alarmed. "What's the matter?"

"The quilt," she whispered.

Shaking his head, he glanced at it, rubbed his face, and returned his gaze to hers. "What, baby? What is it?"

"Nana's wedding quilt. This wasn't on the bed when we came up here! It always stays in her room."

Franklin jumped out of his side of the bed, and quickly drew on his sweat pants and a tee-shirt, and found his sneakers. Colette found her nightgown, robe, and slippers, and they both headed for the door, paused briefly to inspect the lock, then raced down to the kitchen.

"You thinkin' what I'm thinkin'?" he exclaimed, as they flipped on the lights on their way through the house.

Both stopped and looked at each other as they entered the room of destination, then stared wide-eyed at the new, unopened jar of peach preserves that sat on the counter.

"I'm calling Girard," she whispered, but did not move. "We can't sell the house."

"No lie," Franklin affirmed, "call every dag-gone body."

He stood beside her as she dialed the numbers, and woke up the clan one by one, navigating calls past sleepy and curious front desk clerks, all of whom wanted to chat and felt they had a right to—because they knew the family well. She kept her information exchange brief; get home quick, Nana's leaving signs. Then they sat and waited in the parlor, neither one saying a word.

The sound of Juney's plow truck coming down the road was a welcomed noise that made them hurry in unison to the front porch. When the motor idled, Colette turned the door lock and opened it, not allowing Franklin to get far from her side.

Impervious to the cold, they watched him come up the steps to the door, holding a basket very carefully, along with a pink bag over his shoulder. Colette squeezed Franklin's hand, and squinted as a caravan of headlights began to make their way down the road in the distance.

"Look, I know this is a terrible inconvenience, but I didn't know where else to go," Juney said quietly, refusing to come into the house as he thrust the basket forward to Franklin, and handed the pink bag to Colette when she opened the screen door. "Mom, don't look too good. I think her sugar's up…so, I need to take her down to see Doc Pearson, and Cherl's got the kids over at her mother's across town. Too cold, Mom said, to take her all around in a truck in the snow…and Mom said if Jesus call her, that Girard is a lawyer, might know some people who would want a little lamb like this." Apology etched across Juney's ashen face. "Me and Cheri can't barely manage wit the ones we got, so—"

"—Oh, Lord above…" Colette whispered, dropping the diaper bag, and hushing Juney with a kiss. "You tell your Momma that this chile will be looked after by Johnsons, and she don't have to worry about nothin' but getting herself better."

Juney extended his hand to Franklin, and gave Colette a hug before he backed out of the doorway. "Y'all always been good people, 'Lette. You and Frankie both. Much obliged. I gotta get Mom to the doctor's."

She watched him leave, and waved at Miss Julia, who she knew could see her from the truck, then closed the door, gathering up the little bundle within the basket, and pressing her cheek to the sleepy face as it yawned.

"Colette…a baby?"

"Oh, Franklin," she whispered, "look at her…"

He peered inside the blanket and immediately the child reached for his finger, and wrapped its fist around the thick, rough appendage and tried to suckle it.

"Look at this pretty little girl," he whispered in awe. "So delicate…who could leave a child like this?"

Tears filled her eyes, and she kissed her husband's brow. "This house has been giving everybody what they needed, not what they wanted—and she's been keeping it in order, cleaned, just like she used to prepare for all of us coming home for the holidays. Miss Julia said neither she, nor Juney, nor Miss Pat did it. Don't you see the blessings?"

Franklin didn't comment, but cast her an uneasy glance as his line of vision traveled over his shoulder.

"There's nothing to be afraid of, honey," she soothed with confidence. "Nana gave you another taste of her sweetness to remember—in those mysteriously appearing jars of peaches—even though Miss Julia said she'd only canned berries this year. Then she gave Nicole her pictures, and me a taste of history in Miss Julia's kitchen to share with my sister. My cousin, Wilton, and his wife, Deidre, got a christening gown—to let them know that there was no need to worry, and their baby would be born and live. She gave my cousin, Bey, a reminder—her silver heart and Grand Daddy's gold watch, to be sure he knew that he was loved by both her and Pop, and that he was a sibling, not just a cousin. She gave us her quilt, the one that was her wedding quilt…for good luck in making our own babies. But, this child is for Brother and Nancy. This little thing was here when she passed on, probably the last living soul to see Nana alive…here, in this house, just like this little girl was already family. It's a good sign. Trust me."

He stared at her and his eyes misted, then cleared as he looked from her to the baby and back. "That's the only right thing to do, honey. We've got time to wait for our blessings. They don't."

They both chuckled as the baby began to wiggle and kick, making little grunting sounds of hunger on its way to a full-blown wail.

"Go sit on the couch out of the draft, and see if Miss Julia packed some formula. I'll crack the door open, 'cause everybody just pulled up."

Girard was the first one through the door, followed by Bey, then Wilton, with the women all following in a terrified-looking huddle of humanity behind them.

"Nancy, Girard," Colette whispered, "look what Nana gave you for Christmas," she beamed as they approached her on the sofa.

"What?" Nancy whispered back, tears rising and streaming down her face when Colette handed the child out to her to hold.

Girard laced his arm around Nancy's waist, and all the family members fought to get a good look at the wriggling bundle of life.

Nicole whispered, "Nana's in this house, isn't she?" Franklin nodded, and his admission of belief sent a collective gasp through the women in the room.

"All the gifts…everything being just what was the true sentimental thing for each person," Deidre whispered, covering her mouth.

"Whose baby is it?" Sandra whispered, "Somebody just left it, like that—out in the snow?"

"Appears old Miss Davis took a turn this mornin'," Franklin said in a low, serious voice. "Sent Juney by here with this baby for the family to watch, and said to give these papers to Girard." He handed Girard a manila envelope, and proceeded to hug him as he accepted it. "Me and Colette couldn't think of a better father and mother in the family…so…" he shrugged, "Merry Christmas, Daddy."

Girard went over to the armchair, sat down, and covered his face with his hands and wept quietly.

Nancy drew to his side, and knelt before him, placing the baby on his lap.

"Tell them all what we talked about in bed last night," Nancy murmured, kissing her husband's hands until he removed them from his eyes.

"We thought," Girard said in an unsteady voice, "that the house should stay in the family...and, Nicole should have all the pictures—like Mom Johnson would have wanted. And, Bey should have a lot of Pop's things, because Pop was like a father to him. And, Wilton and Deidre should have the baby things, all those handmade toys, and crib, and bassinet...but, the house, should be filled with love, and someone sentimental...with a good woman and a good man that knows how to fix things, and care for more than things—that's Colette and Franklin. Y'all take it. Case closed," he quietly added, allowing the baby to suckle his finger tip. "'Cause, if it wasn't for my sister..." his voice trailed off, "Wouldn't be no glue left to hold this family tight."

"Girard," Franklin protested. "We got a house up in Philly, and I've got an auto-body business to run."

"Ain't no argument to it," Nicole fussed with a smile. "Nana left the signs. Like Girard said, case closed."

"And," Bey protested, "you got a barn out back, that would make an excellent recreation center, if fixed up. Lord knows, we did some recreatin' out there in our day," he laughed, pulling Sandra to him.

"And, there's the big, ole shed," Wilton added, "that could use some equipment to teach vo-tech skills to these young boys in town."

"Who might get a scholarship from a historically black college or a university, if there was an after-school program that could help both the girls and the boys get prepared," Deidre added with a wide grin. "I think my people can see to that."

"And," Nicole chuckled, "there might be a news correspondent that might be able to get the program some national recognition and media attention, which could help ensure solid grants to run the place."

"And," Nancy nodded, taking the baby from Girard to walk around the room, bouncing the infant on her shoulder, "I'm sure that an influential attorney could do the 501c3 paperwork to establish the non-profit…and a well-orchestrated letter-writing campaign from several well-respected black women's organizations, could ensure foundation support in this historic black enclave…which would definitely call for documentary attention," she said, smiling in Nicole's direction.

"No doubt," Girard murmured from his chair, "that well-placed political connections could even coax private contributions for a school bus, and to hire a local driver, like Juney, and to get in solid speakers. But, I'm sure that a good attorney could also negotiate a stellar sales price on a thriving Philadelphia-based auto-body business, enough to install state-of-the-art new equipment in a vocational training center…and that same attorney could reasonably manage row house rental property."

"Yes," Bey chimed in, "might even find that a dental facility might open in town, to assist with internships and teaching office management and dental technician skills, if he retained the proper office manager to support his efforts. You never know." Bey smiled and looked at Sandra, who looked away and giggled.

Suggestions rang out amid Colette and Franklin's feeble protests, until a small wail brought the group to harmonious laughter that trailed them all as they went into the kitchen.

Colette stood at the sink, her eyes shining with tears of gratitude and joy. Franklin absorbed her against his body like hot butter on warm baked bread. Nancy nursed the baby with such tenderness that the group fell silent for a moment while Girard stroked the dark, tight ringlets of infant hair in pure awe. Wilton touched his wife's stomach and nuzzled against her.

"Marry me," Bey said quietly against Sandra's cheek. When she filled his arms, Nicole squealed, and another round of commotion broke out as everyone tried to talk at once.

"I say we all stay here for Christmas," Nicole whimpered, crying as she danced between each couple. "We been blessed…don't you feel the energy in this house? I've gotta get this on tape."

They all agreed, while laughing and bumping into each other, hugging and kissing, and talking a mile a minute. But then, Franklin held up his hand, and the group settled into silent expectation.

"I say before we do anything, we say a prayer of thanks." He looked around the room at all the faces that had become riveted on him.

"I stand down, Franklin Morris," Girard whispered. "It's all yours, brother."

Franklin cleared his throat and bowed his head, holding Colette against him. "May God bless Mom and Pop Johnson for their wisdom, courage, and the spirit of love that they shared…and we thank you Heavenly Father above, for all the true gifts of immeasurable value that you have bestowed upon this family. And, we thank you for allowing us to finally give back the gift of collective effort and harmony and love to those already gone home to Glory. And, I thank you, for giving me back my wife—along with a way to fulfill all of our hopes and dreams…Merry Christmas."

"Merry Christmas," Colette whispered, an instant before she met her husband's lips with her own, sealing their hearts and their future.

2009 Reprint Mass Market Titles

January

I'm Gonna Make You Love Me
Gwyneth Bolton
ISBN-13: 978-1-58571-291-5
ISBN-10: 1-58571-291-4
$6.99

Shades of Desire
Monica White
ISBN-13: 978-1-58571-292-2
ISBN-10: 1-58571-292-2
$6.99

February

A Love of Her Own
Cheris Hodges
ISBN-13: 978-1-58571-293-9
ISBN-10: 1-58571-293-0
$6.99

Color of Trouble
Dyanne Davis
ISBN-13: 978-1-58571-294-6
ISBN-10: 1-58571-096-6
$6.99

March

Twist of Fate
Beverly Clark
ISBN-13: 978-1-58571-295-3
ISBN-10: 1-58571-295-7
$6.99

Chances
Pamela Leigh Starr
ISBN-13: 978-1-58571-296-0
ISBN-10: 1-58571-296-5
$6.99

April

Sinful Intentions
Crystal Rhodes
ISBN-13: 978-1-585712-297-7
ISBN-10: 1-58571-297-3
$6.99

Rock Star
Roslyn Hardy Holcomb
ISBN-13: 978-1-58571-298-4
$6.99

May

Path of Fire
T.T. Henderson
ISBN-13: 978-1-58571-343-1
ISBN-10: 1-58571-343-0
$6.99

Caught Up in the Rapture
Lisa Riley
ISBN-13: 978-1-58571-344-8
ISBN-10: 1-58571-344-9
$6.99

June

Reckless Surrender
Rochelle Alers
ISBN-13: 978-1-58571-345-5
ISBN-10: 1-58571-345-7
$6.99

No Ordinary Love
Angela Weaver
ISBN-13: 978-1-58571-346-2
ISBN-10: 1-58571-346-5
$6.99

2009 Reprint Mass Market Titles (continued)

July

Intentional Mistakes
Michele Sudler
ISBN-13: 978-1-58571-347-9
ISBN-10: 1-58571-347-3
$6.99

It's in His Kiss
Reon Carter
ISBN-13: 978-1-58571-348-6
ISBN-10: 1-58571-348-1
$6.99

August

Unfinished Love Affair
Barbara Keaton
ISBN-13: 978-1-58571-349-3
ISBN-10: 1-58571-349-X
$6.99

A Perfect Place to Pray
I.L Goodwin
ISBN-13: 978-1-58571-299-1
ISBN-10: 1-58571-299-X
$6.99

September

Love in High Gear
Charlotte Roy
ISBN-13: 978-1-58571-355-4
ISBN-10: 1-58571-355-4
$6.99

Ebony Eyes
Kei Swanson
ISBN-13: 978-1-58571-356-1
ISBN-10: 1-58571-356-2
$6.99

October

Midnight Clear
Leslie Esdaile/Carmen Green
ISBN-13: 978-1-58571-357-8
ISBN-10: 1-58571-357-0
$6.99

Midnight Clear, Too
Gwynne Forster/Monica
 Jackson
ISBN-13: 978-1-58571-358-5
ISBN-10: 1-58571-358-9
$6.99

November

Midnight Peril
Vicki Andrews
ISBN-13: 978-1-58571-359-2
ISBN-10: 1-58571-359-7
$6.99

One Day at a Time
Bella McFarland
ISBN-13: 978-1-58571-360-8
ISBN-10: 1-58571-360-0
$6.99

December

Just an Affair
Eugenia O'Neal
ISBN-13: 978-1-58571-361-5
ISBN-10: 1-58571-361-9
$6.99

Shades of Brown
Denise Becker
ISBN-13: 978-1-58571-362-2
ISBN-10: 1-58571-362-7
$6.99

2009 New Mass Market Titles

January

Singing A Song…
Crystal Rhodes
ISBN-13: 978-1-58571-283-0
$6.99

Look Both Ways
Joan Early
ISBN-13: 978-1-58571-284-7
$6.99

February

Six O'Clock
Katrina Spencer
ISBN-13: 978-1-58571-285-4
$6.99

Red Sky
Renee Alexis
ISBN-13: 978-1-58571-286-1
$6.99

March

Anything But Love
Celya Bowers
ISBN-13: 978-1-58571-287-8
$6.99

Tempting Faith
Crystal Hubbard
ISBN-13: 978-1-58571-288-5
$6.99

April

If I Were Your Woman
LaConnie Taylor-Jones
ISBN-13: 978-1-58571-289-2
$6.99

Best of Luck Elsewhere
Trisha Haddad
ISBN-13: 978-1-58571-290-8
$6.99

May

All I'll Ever Need
Mildred Riley
ISBN-13: 978-1-58571-335-6
$6.99

A Place Like Home
Alicia Wiggins
ISBN-13: 978-1-58571-336-3
$6.99

June

Best Foot Forward
Michele Sudler
ISBN-13: 978-1-58571-337-0
$6.99

It's n the Rhythm
Sammie Ward
ISBN-13: 978-1-58571-338-7
$6.99

2009 New Mass Market Titles (continued)

July

Checks and Balances
Elaine Sims
ISBN-13: 978-1-58571-339-4
$6.99

Save Me
Africa Fine
ISBN-13: 978-1-58571-340-0
$6.99

August

When Lightening Strikes
Michele Cameron
ISBN-13: 978-1-58571-369-1
$6.99

Blindsided
Tammy Williams
ISBN-13: 978-1-58571-342-4
$6.99

September

2 Good
Celya Bowers
ISBN-13: 978-1-58571-350-9
$6.99

Waiting for Mr. Darcy
Chamein Canton
ISBN-13: 978-1-58571-351-6
$6.99

October

Fireflies
Joan Early
ISBN-13: 978-1-58571-352-3
$6.99

Frost On My Window
Angela Weaver
ISBN-13: 978-1-58571-353-0
$6.99

November

Waiting in the Shadows
Michele Sudler
ISBN-13: 978-1-58571-364-6
$6.99

Fixin' Tyrone
Keith Walker
ISBN-13: 978-1-58571-365-3
$6.99

December

Dream Keeper
Gail McFarland
ISBN-13: 978-1-58571-366-0
$6.99

Another Memory
Pamela Ridley
ISBN-13: 978-1-58571-367-7
$6.99

Other Genesis Press, Inc. Titles

A Dangerous Deception	J.M. Jeffries	$8.95
A Dangerous Love	J.M. Jeffries	$8.95
A Dangerous Obsession	J.M. Jeffries	$8.95
A Drummer's Beat to Mend	Kei Swanson	$9.95
A Happy Life	Charlotte Harris	$9.95
A Heart's Awakening	Veronica Parker	$9.95
A Lark on the Wing	Phyliss Hamilton	$9.95
A Love of Her Own	Cheris F. Hodges	$9.95
A Love to Cherish	Beverly Clark	$8.95
A Risk of Rain	Dar Tomlinson	$8.95
A Taste of Temptation	Reneé Alexis	$9.95
A Twist of Fate	Beverly Clark	$8.95
A Voice Behind Thunder	Carrie Elizabeth Greene	$6.99
A Will to Love	Angie Daniels	$9.95
Acquisitions	Kimberley White	$8.95
Across	Carol Payne	$12.95
After the Vows	Leslie Esdaile	$10.95
(Summer Anthology)	T.T. Henderson	
	Jacqueline Thomas	
Again, My Love	Kayla Perrin	$10.95
Against the Wind	Gwynne Forster	$8.95
All I Ask	Barbara Keaton	$8.95
Always You	Crystal Hubbard	$6.99
Ambrosia	T.T. Henderson	$8.95
An Unfinished Love Affair	Barbara Keaton	$8.95
And Then Came You	Dorothy Elizabeth Love	$8.95
Angel's Paradise	Janice Angelique	$9.95
At Last	Lisa G. Riley	$8.95
Best of Friends	Natalie Dunbar	$8.95
Beyond the Rapture	Beverly Clark	$9.95
Blame It on Paradise	Crystal Hubbard	$6.99
Blaze	Barbara Keaton	$9.95
Bliss, Inc.	Chamein Canton	$6.99
Blood Lust	J.M.Jeffries	$9.95
Blood Seduction	J.M. Jeffries	$9.95
Bodyguard	Andrea Jackson	$9.95
Boss of Me	Diana Nyad	$8.95
Bound by Love	Beverly Clark	$8.95
Breeze	Robin Hampton Allen	$10.95

Other Genesis Press, Inc. Titles (continued)

Broken	Dar Tomlinson	$24.95
By Design	Barbara Keaton	$8.95
Cajun Heat	Charlene Berry	$8.95
Careless Whispers	Rochelle Alers	$8.95
Cats & Other Tales	Marilyn Wagner	$8.95
Caught in a Trap	Andre Michelle	$8.95
Caught Up in the Rapture	Lisa G. Riley	$9.95
Cautious Heart	Cheris F. Hodges	$8.95
Chances	Pamela Leigh Starr	$8.95
Cherish the Flame	Beverly Clark	$8.95
Choices	Tammy Williams	$6.99
Class Reunion	Irma Jenkins/	$12.95
	John Brown	
Code Name: Diva	J.M. Jeffries	$9.95
Conquering Dr. Wexler's	Kimberley White	$9.95
Heart		
Corporate Seduction	A.C. Arthur	$9.95
Crossing Paths,	Dorothy Elizabeth Love	$9.95
Tempting Memories		
Crush	Crystal Hubbard	$9.95
Cypress Whisperings	Phyllis Hamilton	$8.95
Dark Embrace	Crystal Wilson Harris	$8.95
Dark Storm Rising	Chinelu Moore	$10.95
Daughter of the Wind	Joan Xian	$8.95
Dawn's Harbor	Kymberly Hunt	$6.99
Deadly Sacrifice	Jack Kean	$22.95
Designer Passion	Dar Tomlinson	$8.95
	Diana Richeaux	
Do Over	Celya Bowers	$9.95
Dream Runner	Gail McFarland	$6.99
Dreamtective	Liz Swados	$5.95
Ebony Angel	Deatri King-Bey	$9.95
Ebony Butterfly II	Delilah Dawson	$14.95
Echoes of Yesterday	Beverly Clark	$9.95
Eden's Garden	Elizabeth Rose	$8.95
Eve's Prescription	Edwina Martin Arnold	$8.95
Everlastin' Love	Gay G. Gunn	$8.95
Everlasting Moments	Dorothy Elizabeth Love	$8.95
Everything and More	Sinclair Lebeau	$8.95

Other Genesis Press, Inc. Titles (continued)

Everything But Love	Natalie Dunbar	$8.95
Falling	Natalie Dunbar	$9.95
Fate	Pamela Leigh Starr	$8.95
Finding Isabella	A.J. Garrotto	$8.95
Forbidden Quest	Dar Tomlinson	$10.95
Forever Love	Wanda Y. Thomas	$8.95
From the Ashes	Kathleen Suzanne	$8.95
	Jeanne Sumerix	
Gentle Yearning	Rochelle Alers	$10.95
Glory of Love	Sinclair LeBeau	$10.95
Go Gentle Into That	Malcom Boyd	$12.95
Good Night		
Goldengroove	Mary Beth Craft	$16.95
Groove, Bang, and Jive	Steve Cannon	$8.99
Hand in Glove	Andrea Jackson	$9.95
Hard to Love	Kimberley White	$9.95
Hart & Soul	Angie Daniels	$8.95
Heart of the Phoenix	A.C. Arthur	$9.95
Heartbeat	Stephanie Bedwell-Grime	$8.95
Hearts Remember	M. Loui Quezada	$8.95
Hidden Memories	Robin Allen	$10.95
Higher Ground	Leah Latimer	$19.95
Hitler, the War, and the Pope	Ronald Rychiak	$26.95
How to Write a Romance	Kathryn Falk	$18.95
I Married a Reclining Chair	Lisa M. Fuhs	$8.95
I'll Be Your Shelter	Giselle Carmichael	$8.95
I'll Paint a Sun	A.J. Garrotto	$9.95
Icie	Pamela Leigh Starr	$8.95
Illusions	Pamela Leigh Starr	$8.95
Indigo After Dark Vol. I	Nia Dixon/Angelique	$10.95
Indigo After Dark Vol. II	Dolores Bundy/	$10.95
	Cole Riley	
Indigo After Dark Vol. III	Montana Blue/	$10.95
	Coco Morena	
Indigo After Dark Vol. IV	Cassandra Colt/	$14.95
Indigo After Dark Vol. V	Delilah Dawson	$14.95
Indiscretions	Donna Hill	$8.95
Intentional Mistakes	Michele Sudler	$9.95
Interlude	Donna Hill	$8.95

Other Genesis Press, Inc. Titles (continued)

Intimate Intentions	Angie Daniels	$8.95
It's Not Over Yet	J.J. Michael	$9.95
Jolie's Surrender	Edwina Martin-Arnold	$8.95
Kiss or Keep	Debra Phillips	$8.95
Lace	Giselle Carmichael	$9.95
Lady Preacher	K.T. Richey	$6.99
Last Train to Memphis	Elsa Cook	$12.95
Lasting Valor	Ken Olsen	$24.95
Let Us Prey	Hunter Lundy	$25.95
Lies Too Long	Pamela Ridley	$13.95
Life Is Never As It Seems	J.J. Michael	$12.95
Lighter Shade of Brown	Vicki Andrews	$8.95
Looking for Lily	Africa Fine	$6.99
Love Always	Mildred E. Riley	$10.95
Love Doesn't Come Easy	Charlyne Dickerson	$8.95
Love Unveiled	Gloria Greene	$10.95
Love's Deception	Charlene Berry	$10.95
Love's Destiny	M. Loui Quezada	$8.95
Love's Secrets	Yolanda McVey	$6.99
Mae's Promise	Melody Walcott	$8.95
Magnolia Sunset	Giselle Carmichael	$8.95
Many Shades of Gray	Dyanne Davis	$6.99
Matters of Life and Death	Lesego Malepe, Ph.D.	$15.95
Meant to Be	Jeanne Sumerix	$8.95
Midnight Clear	Leslie Esdaile	$10.95
(Anthology)	Gwynne Forster	
	Carmen Green	
	Monica Jackson	
Midnight Magic	Gwynne Forster	$8.95
Midnight Peril	Vicki Andrews	$10.95
Misconceptions	Pamela Leigh Starr	$9.95
Moments of Clarity	Michele Cameron	$6.99
Montgomery's Children	Richard Perry	$14.95
Mr. Fix-It	Crystal Hubbard	$6.99
My Buffalo Soldier	Barbara B.K. Reeves	$8.95
Naked Soul	Gwynne Forster	$8.95
Never Say Never	Michele Cameron	$6.99
Next to Last Chance	Louisa Dixon	$24.95
No Apologies	Seressia Glass	$8.95

Other Genesis Press, Inc. Titles (continued)

No Commitment Required	Seressia Glass	$8.95
No Regrets	Mildred E. Riley	$8.95
Not His Type	Chamein Canton	$6.99
Nowhere to Run	Gay G. Gunn	$10.95
O Bed! O Breakfast!	Rob Kuehnle	$14.95
Object of His Desire	A.C. Arthur	$8.95
Office Policy	A.C. Arthur	$9.95
Once in a Blue Moon	Dorianne Cole	$9.95
One Day at a Time	Bella McFarland	$8.95
One of These Days	Michele Sudler	$9.95
Outside Chance	Louisa Dixon	$24.95
Passion	T.T. Henderson	$10.95
Passion's Blood	Cherif Fortin	$22.95
Passion's Furies	AlTonya Washington	$6.99
Passion's Journey	Wanda Y. Thomas	$8.95
Past Promises	Jahmel West	$8.95
Path of Fire	T.T. Henderson	$8.95
Path of Thorns	Annetta P. Lee	$9.95
Peace Be Still	Colette Haywood	$12.95
Picture Perfect	Reon Carter	$8.95
Playing for Keeps	Stephanie Salinas	$8.95
Pride & Joi	Gay G. Gunn	$8.95
Promises Made	Bernice Layton	$6.99
Promises to Keep	Alicia Wiggins	$8.95
Quiet Storm	Donna Hill	$10.95
Reckless Surrender	Rochelle Alers	$6.95
Red Polka Dot in a World Full of Plaid	Varian Johnson	$12.95
Reluctant Captive	Joyce Jackson	$8.95
Rendezvous With Fate	Jeanne Sumerix	$8.95
Revelations	Cheris F. Hodges	$8.95
Rivers of the Soul	Leslie Esdaile	$8.95
Rocky Mountain Romance	Kathleen Suzanne	$8.95
Rooms of the Heart	Donna Hill	$8.95
Rough on Rats and Tough on Cats	Chris Parker	$12.95
Secret Library Vol. 1	Nina Sheridan	$18.95
Secret Library Vol. 2	Cassandra Colt	$8.95
Secret Thunder	Annetta P. Lee	$9.95

Other Genesis Press, Inc. Titles (continued)

Shades of Brown	Denise Becker	$8.95
Shades of Desire	Monica White	$8.95
Shadows in the Moonlight	Jeanne Sumerix	$8.95
Sin	Crystal Rhodes	$8.95
Small Whispers	Annetta P. Lee	$6.99
So Amazing	Sinclair LeBeau	$8.95
Somebody's Someone	Sinclair LeBeau	$8.95
Someone to Love	Alicia Wiggins	$8.95
Song in the Park	Martin Brant	$15.95
Soul Eyes	Wayne L. Wilson	$12.95
Soul to Soul	Donna Hill	$8.95
Southern Comfort	J.M. Jeffries	$8.95
Southern Fried Standards	S.R. Maddox	$6.99
Still the Storm	Sharon Robinson	$8.95
Still Waters Run Deep	Leslie Esdaile	$8.95
Stolen Memories	Michele Sudler	$6.99
Stories to Excite You	Anna Forrest/Divine	$14.95
Storm	Pamela Leigh Starr	$6.99
Subtle Secrets	Wanda Y. Thomas	$8.95
Suddenly You	Crystal Hubbard	$9.95
Sweet Repercussions	Kimberley White	$9.95
Sweet Sensations	Gwyneth Bolton	$9.95
Sweet Tomorrows	Kimberly White	$8.95
Taken by You	Dorothy Elizabeth Love	$9.95
Tattooed Tears	T. T. Henderson	$8.95
The Color Line	Lizzette Grayson Carter	$9.95
The Color of Trouble	Dyanne Davis	$8.95
The Disappearance of Allison Jones	Kayla Perrin	$5.95
The Fires Within	Beverly Clark	$9.95
The Foursome	Celya Bowers	$6.99
The Honey Dipper's Legacy	Myra Pannell-Allen	$14.95
The Joker's Love Tune	Sidney Rickman	$15.95
The Little Pretender	Barbara Cartland	$10.95
The Love We Had	Natalie Dunbar	$8.95
The Man Who Could Fly	Bob & Milana Beamon	$18.95
The Missing Link	Charlyne Dickerson	$8.95
The Mission	Pamela Leigh Starr	$6.99
The More Things Change	Chamein Canton	$6.99

Other Genesis Press, Inc. Titles (continued)

The Perfect Frame	Beverly Clark	$9.95
The Price of Love	Sinclair LeBeau	$8.95
The Smoking Life	Ilene Barth	$29.95
The Words of the Pitcher	Kei Swanson	$8.95
Things Forbidden	Maryam Diaab	$6.99
This Life Isn't Perfect Holla	Sandra Foy	$6.99
Three Doors Down	Michele Sudler	$6.99
Three Wishes	Seressia Glass	$8.95
Ties That Bind	Kathleen Suzanne	$8.95
Tiger Woods	Libby Hughes	$5.95
Time Is of the Essence	Angie Daniels	$9.95
Timeless Devotion	Bella McFarland	$9.95
Tomorrow's Promise	Leslie Esdaile	$8.95
Truly Inseparable	Wanda Y. Thomas	$8.95
Two Sides to Every Story	Dyanne Davis	$9.95
Unbreak My Heart	Dar Tomlinson	$8.95
Uncommon Prayer	Kenneth Swanson	$9.95
Unconditional Love	Alicia Wiggins	$8.95
Unconditional	A.C. Arthur	$9.95
Undying Love	Renee Alexis	$6.99
Until Death Do Us Part	Susan Paul	$8.95
Vows of Passion	Bella McFarland	$9.95
Wedding Gown	Dyanne Davis	$8.95
What's Under Benjamin's Bed	Sandra Schaffer	$8.95
When a Man Loves a Woman	LaConnie Taylor-Jones	$6.99
When Dreams Float	Dorothy Elizabeth Love	$8.95
When I'm With You	LaConnie Taylor-Jones	$6.99
Where I Want To Be	Maryam Diaab	$6.99
Whispers in the Night	Dorothy Elizabeth Love	$8.95
Whispers in the Sand	LaFlorya Gauthier	$10.95
Who's That Lady?	Andrea Jackson	$9.95
Wild Ravens	AlTonya Washington	$9.95
Yesterday Is Gone	Beverly Clark	$10.95
Yesterday's Dreams, Tomorrow's Promises	Reon Laudat	$8.95
Your Precious Love	Sinclair LeBeau	$8.95

Order Form

Mail to: Genesis Press, Inc.
P.O. Box 101
Columbus, MS 39703

$1 each additional book
Total S & H
Total amount enclosed

Mississippi residents add 7% sales tax

1-888-INDIGO-1

Visit www.genesis-press.com for latest releases and excerpts.